PARADISE & ELSEWHERE

Paradise
&
Elsewhere

Stories

Kathy Page

A JOHN METCALF BOOK

BIBLIOASIS
WINDSOR, ONTARIO

FIRST EDITION

Library and Archives Canada Cataloguing in Publication

Page, Kathy, 1958-, author
Paradise and elsewhere / written by Kathy Page.

Short stories.
Issued in print and electronic formats.
ISBN 978-1-927428-59-7 (pbk.).--ISBN 978-1-927428-60-3 (epub)

I. Title.

PR6066.A325P37 2014   823'.914   C2013-907292-6
                                               C2013-907293-4

Edited by John Metcalf
Copy-edited by Allana Amlin
Typeset by Chris Andrechek
Cover design by Kate Hargreaves
Cover illustration by Stephanie Grogan

Blibioasis acknowledges the ongoing financial support of the Government of Canada through the Canada Council for the Arts, Canadian Heritage, the Canada Book Fund, and the Government of Ontario through the Ontario Arts Council.

PRINTED AND BOUND IN CANADA

Contents

G'Ming

THE VILLAGE LOOKS closer to the road than it is and I see them coming from a long way off, their clothes bright white against the mud and the scrub of the plain. Most often it is a man and a woman together like this; the man has a camera, and both of them wear money belts around their waists. When they reach the path I slip down from the wall. I watch them coming around the twist in the path; they see me, and I smile.

The woman wears big dark glasses: some years the glasses are big, some years small. She carries a plastic bottle of water. You can see the shape of her body beneath her clothes, the damp patches under her arms. The man is thin. He is beginning to go bald, and although he moves loosely he stoops from being tall. He doesn't wear sunglasses and there are lines on his face, whiter than the rest. He smiles right back when he sees me. Normally it is the woman, but today, he is the one, and so we begin:

7

"I offer you a good afternoon."

"To you also," the man replies: he has some of our language, then, but it will not be so much as I have of his. I offer my hand to shake, first to him then to her. The woman makes a noise in her throat. She flaps her other hand around to chase away the small brown flies that come at this time of year; it only makes them worse, but foreigners never see this.

"My name is Aeiu," I tell them. Theirs are Nick and Liz. And now we have made an exchange, which prepares the ground.

"It is beautiful here," she says. Truly, I don't know if it is or it isn't beautiful. There is earth, sun, water, trees. There could be hundreds of places like this.

"Very beautiful," I tell them, as they nod and agree. "And your wife," I say to the man, "she is like a gazelle." And then we walk together, on towards the village.

I am sixteen but I look less so I tell them twelve. I have two younger brothers and one older and one sister, not married. My father's brother is a holy man who does not have to work—people bring him gifts of food and drink—but the rest of us start with the sunrise. I tell them this and they nod hard again when they understand and say "Good." It is not particularly good, it is how things are, here in G'ming, where I live. Though I do not say that.

The mud walls rise higher either side of the track and as we come into the village, the shade grows deeper. Branches hang over the walls, heavy with fruit. The man and the woman look around with big eyes. But they don't

8

look behind and neither do I. I know without looking that by now the others, the little ones, are following us.

"These are pomegranates." I pick one for the woman. "To quench your thirst. Perhaps you would like to buy a basketful? Or maybe some of our pottery, all very cheap."

"We are just walking, thank you," she says. "We are not buying." We come to the centre of the village, where all the paths meet in a star, which is the marketplace every week, busy, busy, busy. But now it is quiet. The sun is almost overhead, no shade, no sounds. They hesitate, aware of the stillness, and then the boys who have been following break suddenly upon us, laughing and shouting.

It would make a good photograph: the two tall ones, the twenty or so smaller ones, somewhere between their knees and their hips in height, jostling, reaching up. Hands to shake. Lots of shaking. Good afternoon, the man and the woman say back, making our sounds strange. And as for myself, a figure between the two heights, I stand for a moment a little apart. The man has his hand in the small of the woman's back. His camera is Minolta.

ARE YOU A GROWING to be a good man, Aeiu, or a bad man? Since my tenth birthday, my father insists that every year I take an offering to his brother, the holy man. If I am honest, I do not like him. He smells like rotting fruit. He tells me that I should think on this question of goodness and badness as many times a day as I can. It is the way to true riches, he says. He sits by the river all day. It seems to me that he has no obligations.

That is not so, Aeiu, he says, his eyes fixed on the distance, even when he looks right into my eyes. As if the distance were inside my head too.

I know only that I am good at doing certain things. This.

The kids hold their hands out. "Aeiki!" they say, first one, then the rest.

"No aeiki," the man says, loudly shaking his head, but smiling still.

"Aeiki, one aeiki. One dollar!" They cluster around so it is hard to walk and the woman looks back along the track they came down, as if she wants to return. Instead, they veer right, away from the village and down towards the river. We all follow.

"No," the man says. He puts his hand in his pockets and pulls the linings out. Uuio comes forward. He has greasy white cream on the patch of skin on his forehead, and the dust has stuck to it. He taps the man's pouch, and we can all hear the ringing of coins inside.

"Aeiki," he says. But the man, still smiling, shakes his head. And because so far I have asked for nothing, he looks to me for help.

"There are twenty aeiki to one dollar," I say, and shrug, as if to say it is nothing to do with me.

"But why?" the man says, turning back to the kids. "Why aeiki?" So very stupid.

"Aeiki, dollar, aeiki!" they call back.

THE TREES STOP SUDDENLY and the path finishes at the river, where the women are washing clothes and all the coloured things are spread out to dry on the bushes. They stop work and stare back and some of them cover their faces. The kids are asking for pens now, or sweets; they try different languages:

"Stylo, bonbons!" They mime writing, eating, hunger.

"We have nothing," the woman says. A lie. Does she think we have no eyes? She has folded her arms across her chest. They want to be friendly without giving. But this is not possible: why do they think they can pretend a walk here is the same as a walk in their own village? Do they truly expect to come here for nothing? They are seeing my home: they have already had what they wanted. I will never be able to see the place they come from, to walk around it, looking. I do not have a picture of it in my mind, unless it is New York, Hong Kong, or London.

"Aeiki, pen, dollar, Coca-Cola, aeiki, stylo."

"It is beautiful here," I remind them. "Maybe you can take a photograph."

They look at each other quickly. "No, no, no," the man says. "No photographs." But Eeiu and Aui come forward to put their arms around the woman, one each side, and rest their heads on her waist.

"Photo!" they cry.

"No photo."

"Photo!"

"Their poor teeth," the woman says.

"No photograph. Camera finished!" the man says, making a gesture like scissors with his hands.

Eeiu and Aui hold their pose.

"Ten Aeiki," they say.

"No photograph. No aeiki, no dollar," the man tells them. The woman breaks free and Eaio taps her on the arm: he's the oldest after me, but very thin, and he has a small face that looks as if it has suffered much. He points at her bottle of water, then at his mouth. We have both a river and a well, but this they can't refuse. So he drinks, passes the bottle on. An important step. For a short time, everyone is quiet.

"Aeiki, dollar," the boys begin again as we walk back from the river. Then the man takes the empty bottle back and holds it up.

"Soccer? Football?" he says, looking around, smiling very hard. He kicks the bottle. It doesn't go far. He runs after it and looks back at us, kicks it towards Uuio. Uuio passes to Eaio. Eaio to Oii, who heads it back to Uuio…Others rush forward, passing the bottle to and fro until it is crushed and the man, breathing hard, smiles at the woman, a big smile.

"They're just kids," he says.

We are beyond the marketplace now, following the path. Smaller tracks leave off to either side, like the veins of a leaf. The old men sleep on a bank in the shade of the orange trees. Just like my uncle, the one who is a holy man, old men do not have to work, I tell the tourists.

"Aeiki, dollar, aeiki," someone begins. The man turns and puts his tongue out. He puts his finger in his mouth and pulls it, making a noise like the cork from a bottle. Some of the younger ones do it back. But it doesn't last.

"Come to my house." Uuio mimes setting a cloth on the floor then pouring and drinking tea.

"Hospitality," I explain. "You should accept." And now yet others join us and some of the kids try to chase the newcomers away. The woman notices this.

"It is very kind. We want to be friends, but we do not have time to visit," she says.

"No time? On your holiday?"

"We must leave now." She looks ahead. There are many paths.

"Up to you," I say. I am good at this. I need not hurry, because it will work out for me, either way. If they give to the others, they will also give to me. If they do not give to the others, still, in the end, they will give to me.

"You are in a car?" I ask. The man mimes walking, two fingers on the back of his hand.

"This way for the hotel!" says Uuio. It's the way to his house, of course.

"I think it's this way," the man says to the woman, pointing. They hesitate.

"This way," Uuio insists, which almost always works, but these two walk forward, fast, the way they have chosen. The path turns a blind corner and leads to a bank of sandy scrub and tamarisk trees.

"Come back! This way!" Uuio insists. Again they hesitate, but finally they stride on up the bank, fast as they can, slipping in the sand. Some of the smaller ones drift away now. The rest of us follow. From the top of the bank, across the plain are the two piles of stones that mark the edge of the village's land, and then the road and then the hotel. It is small in the distance but by luck they have chosen the shortest way. We follow quietly for a while as they descend the bank, talking to each other in low voices. Once or twice they check to see if we are still there.

At the stones, we are close behind them again. They turn around together.

"Goodbye," they say, as we gather around. The man points at himself and then the hotel, at us and then the village.

"Goodbye," he repeats. Euu, the smallest of those remaining, reaches up to the woman, his lips puckered for a kiss. She bends down and kisses the air to the side of his cheek: she does not want to do this, I can tell. Others follow and she kisses the air besides all of them. When that is done, the man and the woman wave and say goodbye again. No one moves. We stay surrounding them. There is a moment of silence, then Euu says:

"Just one aeiki, just for me."

"But no," the man says softly, "That's it—don't you see? Not fair." He points at all of us. He looks at me.

"Not *fair*," he says. There is a new expression in his eyes, a kind of burning I can't name.

"Fair?" I say.

"Aeiki—aeiki—aeiki" he says pointing at us all.

"There are twenty aeiki to one dollar," I repeat. Sometimes, when they have been here for a while, they forget this. "It is not much."

"Not much, but—" he points at us again, and then into the distance, towards the city, continuing "aeiki, aeiki, aeiki."

Uuio pushes through the others.

"One dollar to me. Little bit each one," he says, smiling hard as he mimes the cutting up of the coin, as if it were a pie.

14

"*Share?*" the man says, looking hopefully into Uuio's eyes. Uuio nods. The woman says something very fast, her voice sharp. But then she smiles at the man very softly as if he were a child and he opens his money belt. Of course he does not want us to see how much money he has in there, so his fingers are awkward. He pulls out two coins. One he puts in Uuio's hands. The other drops to the ground: everyone fights. Eeai wins it and runs back to the village. Uuio follows. Dust flies up after them.

Aeiki, aeiki, the unlucky ones call. They grasp at the man's legs, reach for the money belt.

"No! That's it! Go away!" he says, pushing the hands away. His voice has changed. He's angry, or something like it. The woman puts her arm through his. They take a few steps. We follow.

"Please!" the woman says over her shoulder. The man does not turn around at all. I go around to the front of them, hold out my hand, to the woman this time, palm up.

"Ten aeiki," I say. "Give me ten aeiki. Then I will make them go."

"What?" she says.

"Ten and I will make them go. And ten for me, for me to go," I say, "twenty in all." I hope they understand how foolish they have been. They could have paid and seen properly, seen inside our houses, taken their pictures, but now they must pay anyway, without doing these things.

"For Chrissake!" The man spins around, opening the pouch as he does. They never have change: it's a fifty aeiki note.

I take it and bow my head as I thank him. I will ride the bus to the town and change the note for smaller currency there. I will keep ten, maybe fifteen for myself and give the rest to my father. I've never told him I do this, but perhaps he knows and says nothing. After all, it was he who stopped me going to school, and I pay my way now. And I honour my bargain with the tourists also; I tell the boys to go and they do. Later I will give them something.

I take one last look at the man, Nick. He stands there with his money belt still open and looks back at me. There is something not right. His face is loose and the eyes in it are shining: the skin under them is wet with tears. He takes a deep breath, turns away. The woman, Liz, reaches up his back, rubs the space between the shoulders and they walk away across the plain. They stay together like that and they do not look back.

DOES THE GOAT CRY when it is milked, or the sheep when shorn? There is no end to the foolishness of the tourist, I think as the bus pulls into the square. And for a man with a belt of money to weep over such a sum is a truly astounding thing. I tell myself this but nonetheless, I prefer a smile and this was not how it was supposed to end and despite myself I keep remembering the man, how he wept and how the woman who seemed so hard before touched him gently between the shoulder blades.

I think of him as I change the fifty note into four tens and ten one aeiki coins. I think how for a few hours I am as rich as him, the tourist. I can go anywhere, eat anything. But only here, in my country. I have never been to any other, and that is why I do not know whether it is beautiful here or not.

A woman sits under the trees in the square, her blind eyes like two half-cooked eggs in her face. She can tell when someone comes near from the sound of their steps and the breeze they make. I give her two aeiki from my part of the money and when I put the two coins right in her hand her fingers close over them fast, as if I might change my mind.

I always do this, and she always says, "Bless you. God will know that you are a good man." But today this leaves me feeling empty. I am still feeling that way, and thinking that I will have a Coca-Cola to fill me up, when I meet the blonde woman, tall, perfect, like an actress from the movies. She wants the bus station, she says. I take her rucksack from her and lead her there, going through the back streets, naturally, because that way it seems longer and more of a service.

"Thank you," she says, standing there where all the buses and people are, her rucksack on the ground, "you are very kind." Her hand moves to the money belt around her waist and I realize then that I need not have taken the long way:

"No," I tell her, "no charge." I pick up the rucksack and walk over to the man who is loading the luggage on to the top of the bus to T'ing. I tell her she must keep the ticket for it safe, and she thanks me again before she climbs on. She waves as her bus sets off.

I SIT BY THE WINDOW on the way home and listen to the music, a song about God, and how he sees into our hearts.

Aieu, I think to myself, just maybe it will be all right if he picks your heart to look into. Right now it feels like a light place, a good place, and I sing along to the words in my head until the coins dig into my hip bone and that makes me think to check my back pocket, where I put the four green ten aeiki notes. I pull them out and then I see that in there with them there is another, a red one, another fifty. The blonde foreigner must have done this as I bent to carry her bag over to the bus. She paid me anyway.

The bus stops by the boulder at the side of the road. As I begin to walk towards the trees that mark the village I find myself thinking how I could open my hand, let her money be picked up and blown in the wind, which is God's will—yet I can't do it. And I can't go home. I look back at the road, and the little puffs of dust that show where the bus is now. Then I think: Fifty aeiki would take me to the border, beyond... But what then? I have no picture in my mind. Still, I do not want to go home, so I pick my way through the narrow paths between the fields, over the planks that cross the irrigation channels, towards the riverbed.

My uncle sits in a small patch of shade on the bank. The whites of his eyes are pink and the rank, sweetish smell is very strong today. The cloths on his head and around his waist are so dirty they are almost the same colour as the earth itself. Yet my father says he is clean in other ways: we must all respect a man who has kept himself free of the flesh. Flies circle him, settle, and he does not move. He is eating an apricot. Beside him are five more, sunset coloured and perfectly ripe, gathered into a small palm basket lined with glossy leaves. A gift. No one else here eats apricots; they are for selling. An aeroplane calls just for them every day.

I sit a distance away. He goes on chewing in his slow, toothless way as I tell him how I saw the two strangers coming, how later I sat on the bus and found the blonde foreigner's money that I did not want, because I wanted to be more than someone she paid to take her bag. At the end of it all, I reach forward to offer my father's brother, the holy man, the fifty aeiki note that she put in my pocket. He looks at it, and then at me; only his eyes move. He shakes his head slowly from side to side, removes the apricot stone from his mouth and throws it in the river. My voice rings out:

"What are you here for, if not to take our gifts?" He looks into the distance inside my head. He picks up the basket, offers me an apricot, which I refuse. He wipes his mouth on his sleeve, tells me:

"You might resolve to keep the fifty Aeiki note without spending it."

"Why? Money must *do* something."

"True," he answers. "It has already." He turns to face the river again, sitting so still that he could be dead. And eventually, I fold the banknote over and over into a small square and tie it tight with a thread from my shirt. I suppose I could make a tiny box for it, and hang it around my neck.

The smells of smoke and of the first evening meals fill the air. I hear rustling, laughter: at this time the unmarried women carry their baskets through the trees to the village, home, where the walls are the colour of mixed spices and the leaves of the trees a very bright green against them. If you are quiet in yourself you can always hear the river, which is very low this year and almost the same red-brown colour as the earth, the walls, the plain. Beyond the plain are the rocks; above them, the sky. There is no space between, none at all. It is here, G'ming, where I will live out my life.

Lak-ha

S TRANGERS ASK WHY people would ever choose to make such a place as this their home: the topsoil is nothing but stones. It drains far too easily and a steady supply of water is impossible to obtain because nine months of the year the sun shines without respite and there is no rain at all. For the other three, torrents fall and temperatures often reach freezing, due to the winds that blow fast and furious from the pole, touching no other patch of ground except that of this remote peninsula. There is no other part of the world, especially so near to sea level, which has such a climate of fire and ice. And, likewise, nowhere else does the Hetlas tree survive, let alone thrive as it does here.

It's short but wide-trunked, a long-living tree, with brief, gnarled branches ending in clusters of dark green, blade-like leaves. The wood is soft and pale, the bark thick and hard. It is because of the Hetlas that we live here.

In the beginning, somehow—propelled, dropped there the way a seed is, who knows—a single family came to be living on this wooded shelf, perched between the terrible mountains and the raging sea. They were hungry all winter, thirsty all summer. Towards summer's end the woman began to weep, desperate to see her husband and two children withering before her eyes. She wept and wept.

"Please stop, oh please stop!" the children pleaded, desperate to see the precious fluid flowing wastefully, undrinkable, from their mother's body. "Stop crying, it will only make you thirstier!"

"For all our sakes, be quiet, be strong!" her husband admonished her. But the woman could not help herself. She sat and wept, her face in her hands, her elbows resting on the rough table made of Hetlas planks. The sound of her moans and her continual sniffing drove her husband and children half-mad and kept them from sleeping. She wept for six days without stopping, until her body was shrivelled and she could weep no more. At last, on the seventh night the family finally slept, but they woke to find the woman dead, and dry as a stick. With the last of their energy they buried her. No one had the strength to mourn.

It was not until the next day that the husband saw the table, which had turned into a skein of fibres blowing in the breeze: the woman's salty tears had washed away all the soft part of the wood, leaving only those parts which are like the veins and arteries of the human body, but much stronger. He carried the fibres out to dry in the sun, and as it happened just then a stranger passed.

"How much do you want for that?" he asked, a greedy gleam in his eyes.

"This?" the man said, puzzled, but sensible enough to pull it back out of reach when the stranger grabbed. "Forty jars of fresh, pure water, and enough food to last the winter out," he said, adding "and another woman, because mine has died."

AFTER THIS, THE FAMILY began to prosper. Mischance had led them to understanding. It was easy to see that just as they lived below the forests, so they also lived above the sea. Every year more strangers came by sea bringing food and goods in exchange for Hetlas rope.

This story explains the name of our village, Lak-ha, which some say means in the old language, "The place where the bargain was struck." Others say other things. They ask, did the woman know the purpose of her weeping? Who invented the Hetlas rope—the woman, the man, the stranger, Fate? But I say, forget it. Come inside. We have everything now: television, internet, iPod, cellphone, denim jeans, Barbie doll, same as you.

Of Paradise

I N THE BEGINNING, we knew our luck: to look through one of the narrow, outer windows upon our fertile land and the desert that lay beyond it was to meditate on our good fortune and on the oppositeness of the world: fullness and emptiness; colour, monochrome; fertility, barrenness, and also upon its miracles: ourselves and however we had come to be, that folding of rocks which provided us with so much wetness, with fruit, grain, wine. Even the miles of burning sand and thorny scrub that separated us from whatever else there might be were a blessing of sorts, for we sensed that there was an else and an other, and also that we should not rush to meet it.

Some say that in those first times we had slowly slipped into a kind of decadence, an exaggerated freedom, and they say that what has come since is some kind of consequence, even a punishment. I'm not convinced. But certainly, back then, we painted our skins and wore our clothes differently every day, we tried always to find new beauty, worried endlessly over a colour or a pattern or the design of a door handle. We studied the sky and thought of new names for its daily different blues. Back then, we were connoisseurs, thinkers, debaters, pluckers of idle but achingly beautiful tunes. We ate at meals and between them, all day, savouring what we had grown and what we could make from it. We were plump and beautiful, with our glossy hair and skin soft and supple from passing so much time in the dappled shade of trees and the softer dimness of our homes. We did not strive, yet were not idle: we gardened, wove, painted—and so the days passed, and then the nights in stargazing, the pleasures of our flesh, dreams.

It was never, as some now say, dull. Nor was it quite perfect. Rivalries developed, occasionally fights. There was once a murder, for which the punishment was a magnificent feast, then execution.

Occasionally during what we now call centuries, some kind of vehicle was glimpsed on the horizon, or even overhead. For days afterwards we would be irritable and anxious, but nothing had ever come of these sightings. It was as if they did not see us and perhaps they truly did not.

One day, though, the baking calm of the desert was disturbed by a moving speck which grew over several hours gradually larger then finally revealed itself to be, so far as we could tell, one of us: two arms, two legs, (though it progressed at least half of the time on all fours). A skin, not smooth and oiled like ours but grained and creased and raging red beneath its layers of dirt: a bit of flesh, just living, that dragged itself towards us across the sand and rock.

At that time there were no city walls. The figure stumbled to the edge of the oasis then knelt on the ground. Someone with a cart picked her up and brought her to the dense shade of the central square, where all of us gathered to watch.

"Water," the traveller said. She said it in her own language, an abrupt, grunting kind of talk—but we knew what she meant and it was already being drawn. We told her our more liquid word for it, and watched as she drained the bowl then sat still on her heels, gripping it. We all felt her thirst, how the coolness of the liquid calmed the burning inside her—even her mind, we knew, would be soothed by the sweet fluid which had seeped for millennia into the basin of rock beneath us. A trickle ran down her chin and neck, and into the dusty hollow at the base of her throat. Her raw lips shone.

"Water," the traveller said again, still in her own tongue, and the bucket was set close by her so that she could fill the bowl herself. "Water!" she shouted after her second drink, and her face cracked into a smile, which we, standing there returned: it is always good to see someone get her relief, whatever it may be. She made to get to her feet, sank down again and plunged her hands into the bucket, splashing the cool liquid over her arms and chest. The faded brown cloth she wore stuck to her flesh, making her seem even thinner than she was, but at the same time her eyes, scoured almost shut by the gritty desert wind, opened a fraction more and we could see that they were green.

We carried her to the pool. She sat for a long time on the side with just her feet in the water, weeping. Then she slipped in by inches. We watched, bewildered and moved: none of us had ever been so dry, so desperate, so alone.

How did she come to be there? Some guessed that she must be some kind of outcast: why else would a person, a bag of water, thinly skinned, wander in an endless burning waste? No one would choose it. Somewhere, to the West, since that was the way she had come, she must have done something terrible enough to be sent away from her people, whoever they were. Had we ourselves not considered exile as a punishment for the murder, but dismissed it as too cruel? But perhaps, others argued, she had simply set out on a journey, as other peoples evidently did, and somehow been left behind by her companions. Did she know we were here? Had she or they even sought us out? How could we know?

It seemed to me that it was as important to be just, as to be careful. How would we ever know the traveller's story, let alone whether or not she was telling the truth? And what would we do with her, seeing as it was surely not possible to throw her back where she came from, unless some kind of guilt could be established?

WHATEVER OUR SPECULATIONS, the traveller certainly did not seem like any kind of threat. In a day or so the sore eyes widened further and brightened, the broken blood vessels healed. Her breath came more regularly. But health was exhausting and every half hour she would curl up and fall asleep. So there was no great urgency to our discussions and we soon grew to enjoy her delight in the abundance that was ordinary for us. We competed for turns at giving her drinks from our most beautiful bowls, and in flavouring the water with fruits and essences. We showered her with clothes and jewellery, and waited to see which she would wear. We studied her to know how to behave for the best, when for example, to leave her in peace, as she seemed easily worn with company and embarrassed by nakedness.

Our suspicions melted. We felt the tug of something like love for the traveller, who had come so far to reach us, was like us, yet was not. We noticed, for instance, how firmly she knew what she wanted and was impossible to persuade, utterly immune to temptation or distraction. For many days she refused all solid food, taking only paps and gruels and that very slowly—so that we took to inventing new recipes with watered milk and pulverized grains and fruit. Just as we had accustomed ourselves to producing these and learned which ones she liked, the traveller began to ask instead for a share of what was on our plates. At this point we understood that she was truly recovered, and opinions began to divide again.

I said that she must be taught our language. Then she could tell us why she was here, and we could decide whether she would stay or not, and if so she would have to be told our methods of cultivation and given a home and responsibilities. Others agreed that she should learn how to speak to us, but only so that we could find out where she had come from and send her back to it; there were limits to hospitality. However well-taught and well-loved she was, these people said, she would always feel slightly apart from us who had always been here. That could make her secretly vengeful, excessively ambitious, or craving of recognition, therefore dangerous.

The truth would take too long to discover, said those who were already convinced she had been exiled for committing some ghastly offence. By the time we were sure of the facts, we would be fond of her and she would in effect be living here already; sending her away would be more painful, but just as necessary. We should simply give her a bag of provisions, they said, and encourage her to continue her journey the next day.

We talked this over in twos or threes in the fields and gardens, we continued in larger groups, between other things, as we sat at table in the evenings. Any opinion that seemed extreme or novel quickly passed by word of mouth and was tested, adopted or rejected by the rest. Back then, we always discussed things minutely, this way and that, taking our time, pondering until some kind of agreement was reached. There is no hurry, we always told each other then, it is a pleasure in any case to talk…And the case of the stranger in the garden was endlessly complicated, or fruitful, depending on how you saw it.

Why were some of us afraid of the traveller? Why did we want to turn aside what fate had sent us? The traveller, I pointed out, might well be a gift as much as a responsibility. She might have some skill we did not practise, she might have reached some understanding we were still groping for. Perhaps we should accept the unfamiliar and learn from it? After all, when occasionally a new plant is found growing in our fields, we discover its properties and decide whether it might be worth cultivating. We do not simply tear it out. Others elaborated this idea, comparing the traveller's differentness to the grains of sand that cause some shelled creatures to grow gemstones inside themselves. How do we know, others countered, that the gemstone is of any value to the animal itself? Indeed the contrary seems more likely when you consider what it is: a hard object, pressing into soft flesh.

Then again, how different was the traveller? She spoke another tongue, was evidently used to other customs; she was flat-chested, had green eyes, and paler, thinner hair but more of it: she was just a little different, not enough to make her completely other. We had recognized her as human from the start. Differentness was not the point, some said. It led both ways. Rather, the issue was that she had come from elsewhere and so we did not know her story or her intentions.

In time many people tired of the discussion, though those who wished her gone were less tired than the rest. Eventually, the one thing that united almost everyone was a feeling that the traveller, who now lay peacefully on our couches, eating pies and pastes and watching us as we talked, even helping with light work, was taking up too much of our attention. I offered to make her my special responsibility, but this, I was told, would not solve the problem, and finally it was indeed decided to send her away.

Two hours before dawn, the sand would be at its coolest. The air, at that time, when the invisible moisture that precipitates in the night has washed it of impediments, is extraordinarily still and clear. The traveller was to be dispatched with as much hospitality as she could carry. We had packed her a bag, making sure to include foods as dense in nutrients as possible and salty enough to counteract sweating, but not so salty as to create excessive thirst: nuts, seedcake, dried fruits, all of it wrapped in scented leaves. Even those who had most wanted the traveller to go softened now that she was about to leave, found themselves wanting her to remember us well. Two skins of water was easy enough for a fit person, as she was now, to carry. We supplied a yoke to make the carrying easier. We made special voluminous robes, a head wrap. A party of six undertook to wake her and lead her out of the oasis, then hand her the provisions and communicate our wishes as best we could.

I was not one of the party but I woke that night at the appointed time, aware of my heart beating hard in my chest. A dog growled low in its throat, preparing for alarm. I heard, or sensed the break in the traveller's breathing in the house next to mine, the rustle of her bedclothes as she sat up. They had agreed to stand back, so that she was not afraid, then to indicate that she must dress and follow them. The light would be snuffed as soon as they emerged, so that everyone's eyes would accustom to the faint radiance preceding the dawn. My favourite time is just a little later in the day, when the colours are newborn. But just before dawn there is a quite different beauty and other senses than sight come to the fore. Perhaps, I thought, the traveller had not experienced the oasis like that before— shades of black and violet against a yellow-grey sky, the air full of whispers and rustling?

The seven of them walked between buildings, across the square and onto the network of paths that cross and link our perennially moist fields. The smells of tomato plants, herbs, melons, and compost rose about them. Dew dropped on their feet. No one said anything: the traveller's vocabulary had not evolved beyond greetings, requests for food and thanks; mainly she relied on facial expressions.

Within half an hour they were at the sand and within half an hour more they had stopped walking. A slice of sun appeared on the rim of the world. The food and drink were handed over, the shadow play ensued. One cast her arm in a circle, so as to indicate: you may go anywhere! Afterwards, this struck us all as ludicrous and faintly shameful. All together they pointed, then pushed her gently on the back. She understood, certainly, the six of them reported back that morning, but what she did was sit down on the sand. To think, we supposed. To remember where it was she had been going to or had come from? In any case, they left her there.

Later that day I was hoeing my melon bed. The scent of ripening fruit was overwhelming and the damp rich earth pushed up between my toes. I was thinking rather sadly about the traveller: how confused she must have felt between our first kindness and her sudden expulsion—when I looked up, and she was there.

In silence, we examined each other. She wore the head cloth we had given her, and the other garment, tied about the waist. She was healthy now, but still not beautiful, I remember thinking: her face and body compelled attention, but it was hard to know how to respond to them;

her features, her coarse skin with its odd growths of hair unsettled, rather than pleased. Nonetheless, I felt drawn to step forward and take her in my arms—a gesture of regret and welcome mixed, I thought, but soon I realized that I felt desire, and looked into her face to see if it was the same for her. I could not tell: her expression at that moment was distant, even though I stood reflected in the pupils of her eyes; I saw, too, a kind of determination that was new to me, though as I looked I felt that the shadow of both these things might well have been present in her face all along. The traveller looked away, and stepped out of my embrace. She nodded in the direction of the houses, walked towards them.

She would not do what we told her to. From that moment on the choice was very stark: we must keep her, or we must kill her; we could not kill her. We knew this, and so did she; everything changed.

Now, she demanded things of us, rather than waiting for us to offer or set out our position. Land; help carrying the stones, branches and hides to build a house; tools, seed. She demanded, we debated whether to give—but the debate was a limited one, and each time we knew sooner that we would give her what she wanted, and soon it became automatic. When the house was built and the field had been levelled and sown, she began properly to learn our language which she then used to ask yet more of us: to learn our stories, songs, musical instruments…Even then the traveller was not content, and wanted to lie with us as we did with each other. It was I who did this first: I saw before anyone else that she had no mouth between her

34

legs, but a thumb-like thing which swelled and grew in a way that to my mind was not entirely foreign, but which, to begin with, filled many of us with fear or disgust.

So I bear the blame. Many people say this physical union was one thing which might have been withheld, had I not set the precedent. But to those of us who did go with her it seemed that at least in this respect she had brought something to us. She fitted inside us and left our hands free to cultivate other gardens, new pleasures…And so after all there was a bargain to be had, we said, though at other times when we looked into her face and saw the set of it as she rubbed the inside of us, however exquisitely, we could equally feel unsettled and afraid. We were used to a passion that was knowing and intimate, but this face was the face of someone on a long and perhaps bitter journey, and only for a moment sometimes as she neared her climax did it soften, before reforming again to a gentler version of its former self: the traveller at the very beginning of her journey, one might say, not yet desperate, but already knowing that she would be so again…This, I privately thought, and not the things we had noticed in the beginning, nor the strange shape of the flesh between her legs, this was the difference we had always sensed.

From it, from the pleasure we made with her, something has lodged in the tender flesh of our commonwealth: the twin pearls of birth and death. The first of these made us more like ourselves; the second made us more like the traveller and that in turn changed everything by degrees. We became the same as the other beings, the birds that passed above and the plants which we grew and ate. And now there is no longer an infinity of time in which to talk and we have never agreed whether it is better or worse to be this way: in either case, we say, that was done, and now this is. The oasis as it used to be is an invisible landscape which we carry buried inside of us and now can reach only rarely, by intricate acts of memory and forgetfulness.

The Ancient Siddanese

OUR GUIDE STEPS FROM the shadows to greet us. He looks cool in his loose white suit and dark glasses; we, fresh from the dark-windowed hover-bug, are reeling in the desert heat.

"Ladies and gentlemen, I don't believe in false modesty so I can tell you that you're fortunate to have me as your official guide for today! Do come inside, out of this terrible heat…" He makes a little bow as he greets us. We eye the Perspex dome behind him suspiciously: the walls of pinkish stone beneath it look squat, plain and, frankly, ugly. It all seems terribly small, set in such an unremitting expanse of space.

"I have spent twenty-three years studying these ruins," our guide continues as we wipe our brows and sigh in the shade of the reception area. He gives the faintest of smiles, "And I'm personally responsible for several of the discoveries which have at last made a definitive interpretation of the site possible. Furthermore, I'm one of the few people who can claim to be descended from the ancient Siddanese themselves…"

Sidda, I've read in the monograph, has been open to the public for over a hundred years, though even now when everyone travels so incessantly, few people arrive here, it being so remote. That's part of the attraction, I suppose. We're an odd group, about fifteen, all different in our ages, nationalities and states of health. But we're all pilgrims of a kind: the couple bent with age, the father with his two sons, the photographer, the three girls, the woman with the baby and the sun-resistant clothes she has designed herself and constantly recommends to the rest of us.

"Everything covered!" she declares proudly. "Even the face. No need for all those chemical creams which are probably as bad for you as the sun itself." She is an optimist, she told me in the hoverbug: "There's always a way."

I suspect I am not the only one who wishes that the fat man with the peppering of dark growths creeping across his face and the backs of his hands would wear her outfit—would tuck the thin silvery veil into his collar, sit his hat back on top, slide his hands into the stretch gloves you can't even feel, and let us all forget. Not that it's easy.

"Before we move out on to the site, I must ask you to change into the soft shoes provided, and warn you about the light here. Despite the dome erected over the site to prevent wind-damage and cut out some of the glare, no one should venture outside without some kind of extra protection, particularly on their head and shoulders. The shading and air conditioning are efficient, but deceptive."

Obediently we re-cream our faces and hands, search for hats and sunglasses in our bags. Except, that is, for Mr. Melanoma, who stands defiant and tries unsuccessfully to catch the guide's eye, as if to say man to man—what a silly, pointless fuss, shutting the stable door, eh?—and the veiled woman, of course, who quickly checks her baby's layers of protection, then waits—serene, I suppose, though, hidden beneath that silvery curtain, she could be weeping for all I really know.

"Terrible thing to do," someone mutters, poking me in the side, "exposing a child like that." I smile and shrug. I don't want to be distracted. I want to get what I came for. Our guide waits, unmoving, until we are finished.

"Despite the discomfort, what you are to see today is certainly absolutely unique and you'll all thank yourselves for having made the effort. Thank you." He makes his bow again. "Come over to the observation panel, please."

There is something about our guide that I like. I'm hopeful. It's a great responsibility, I think, watching how he stands, turning his head smoothly from us to the observation panel and back, telling us of the recent history of the site—as great a responsibility, if not greater than that of the pilot who bore me safely from home to here, speeding between the sun and the too-bright sea. A careless or malicious guide can ruin a trip like this, can leave you with nightmares and a very bitter taste in your mouth.

"Let's begin with an overview."

The party falls silent. Through the tinted pane that makes all colours seem richer than they are, lending the desert an almost damp appearance, a tempting succulence, we gaze at the pinkish stones that are Sidda. Before this one, there have been other guides here, official and unofficial, and before them of course came explorers, those first archaeologists who sought such places out, and they in turn had guides of their own. Now there is him. It is his job to make Sidda complete for us, to add something to the things we can read in books.

"Mr. Sidney Carbourne," he begins, "is credited with the discovery of Sidda…"

TWO MEN, CROSSING THE DESERT. Both wear cloths draped over their heads then wrapped around their necks according to the local custom, but one of them is a European: Mr. Sidney Carbourne, gentleman. Behind the two men, three imported camels, heavily laden—not only with the necessities of life: tents, water, food, but also with notebooks, ink, pens and many lumps of stone.

"What is that, in the distance to the left?" Carbourne asks, gesturing at a small eminence, indistinct and pinkish in the haze of heat.

"To the left, sir?" The other man does not look up; although he knows the desert better than anyone alive, he has never seen it, for he was born blind. Besides, he is old and each journey he makes tires him more. This one he thinks—almost hopes—will be his last.

"That will be the old city of Sidda," he says. "I don't recommend we stop: it's little more than a heap of stones."

"Aha!" Carbourne's voice is always loud, and now it is jubilant as well. Since they set out he has continually suspected his guide of laziness and of trying to cheat him; were the man's eyes not so obviously useless, seamed shut as if by tiny stitches, he would suspect him of counterfeiting his blindness itself. "But that could be said of many sites. You people are so used to the ancient wonders of your land that you often fail to appreciate them. Let us go to Sidda. Perhaps we can camp there for the night."

"It's a long way," the old man says.

"Nonsense!" Carbourne smiles broadly. They have been together four months now. Sometimes he relieves his irritation by making faces at his guide, secure in the knowledge that his rudeness won't be detected. He straightens his back. "Sidda, by nightfall!" he cries.

"It is farther than you think," the old man replies quietly, "and I need to rest." Nonetheless, he alters direction. Carbourne begins to whistle a marching song. By the time it is dark they are perhaps halfway there.

"I presume," Carbourne says, "you can find our way just as well in the dark?"

"Please give me some water," the old man replies. "Yes. Besides, we are going the right way. Our mounts will take us there."

After many hours, through most of which Carbourne has slept, something alerts him to a change and he wakes. The moon has emerged, and they are riding through a walled square. He stops, dismounts, then grabs the halter of his guide's beast.

"Wake up, you!" he shouts at the figure slumped in the saddle. "There's work to be done! I know your game!"

He waits for the figure to start and straighten, but when the camel stamps, it slips further down in the seat. The old man has died, leaving Carbourne to tend the camels, tie them to a crude statue standing in the centre of the square, light a dung fire, unpack blankets and sleep alone till dawn.

When it is light he heaves the body, rigid but very light, from the camel, and carries it to the corner of the square: the death was obviously from the most natural cause of all, and not in any way his fault; the man, he tells himself, is too old to have anyone waiting for his return. Then he wanders around the ruins of Sidda…

"IMMEDIATELY," SAYS OUR GUIDE, gesturing gracefully through the panel, "immediately, you are struck by the central feature: a square of open ground a hundred metres across, bordered by four very thick walls roughly two metres high. Even from here you can see that these walls are in fact even thicker at their base than at the top, and that they're built from irregular but precisely interlocking pieces of pinkish stone. There is no mortar. These stones were mined, shaped and assembled here without the use of any tools other than other pieces of stone. You'll notice that this isn't strictly speaking a square at all, because the four walls do not join at the corners and show no sign of ever having done so. In the centre of the square, where the paths that pass through these openings meet, exactly where it was found, is a large statue made of similar stone but of a greenish hue.

"Beyond the confines of the square you'll notice the seemingly irregular disposition of thirty-nine circular holes

surmounted with low stonework rims. I don't want anyone to try and get inside these holes—they are very deep
indeed and do provide a cool resting place for several types
of snake. Bear in mind that these rims were originally several metres high, but that early explorers of the site were
driven to knock them down in order to make them con-
form to their mistaken notions about the purpose of the
pits. Over there to the left of the site you can see one of the
pit mouths which is in the process of painstaking recon-
struction, and far out on the edge of the site that mound
is where the stones so dishonestly removed were hidden.
Many of these stones were used to construct the base for
the protective dome so as to be in harmony with the site it
protects and also as an experiment to calculate how long it
would have taken to construct Sidda. Our low wall took a
team of twenty men fifteen years to build, using the interlocking method. Sidda was not built in a day!

"Leading up to each of the square's open corners
are what look like narrow roads or paths—these lead
due north, south, east and west, and appear to peter out
just beyond the limits of the site as defined by our dome,
though it's my view that proper exploration would show
them to lead straight on for very many miles. The paths are
made from millions of brittle pottery shards, and among
these have been found many which bear finely preserved
examples of the letters of an ancient alphabet.

"Outside the north, south, west and east walls of the
square you can see the remains of three hexagonal structures. In the southern hexagon were found the only human
remains the site has yielded, and these can now be seen in

the site museum. Now, let us go outside, and I'll tell you a little about the people who constructed Sidda, and the way they lived…"

We follow him out into the tinted dome. You can tell he is right about the sun, for though it is cooler than outside, thin shadows trail behind us and the dry walls are hot to touch. We are a unique generation, skipping as we do from shadow to shadow, our skins screened to escape the fire that once created us. A generation of greedy travellers, living in the last days and wanting to see it all, the world as onion, layer on layer going back beneath today's crisp, dry skin.

SIDNEY CARBOURNE LIVED in a different world and saw different things. He missed the interlocking stones entirely, had not the slightest thought of alphabets. He stepped out protected only by a cotton cloth wrapped over his head. He examined the numerous circular holes in the ground: wells, he thought, now gone dry, and the reason, probably, for the city being abandoned. The hexagonal structures he judged to be fortifications. If the old man had still been with him, he would have pretended a greater interest than he felt, but, alone, he could admit that the city was indeed little more than a heap of stones piled together to form a courtyard—without ornament other than the crude statue. He was disappointed, but there was no point in staying.

It was only as he walked back to the square that he was struck by the enormous thickness of its walls and noticed also that, whereas their inner surface seemed roughly perpendicular, the outer one sloped ever so slightly inwards towards the top. He stood back, shielded his eyes and projected this angle into the sky. The stones of Sidda leapt to life. He saw the place, as new. He stood, filled with it, a great smile carving up his sunburned face.

In a fever of excitement he returned to unload his drawing and measuring instruments. If only he had taken the risk of bringing a whole team out! If only he had more water! If only his guide had not chosen such a moment to die! All day he worked, recording Sidda in plan, section and elevations, all to scale, on fine cartridge paper, his ink drying instantaneously in the heat. Here and there he embellished the scene with a scrubby tree, a lizard or some imaginary birds wheeling in the sky, for it was all rather plain. He drew until dark came, suddenly as it does in these latitudes, then wandered restlessly around the ruins in the dark, feeling the stones, collecting handfuls of pottery shards. It would take him two months to organize a proper expedition and he felt he would be unable to sleep until he returned.

In the morning he spent an hour with his maps and a compass. Sidda was unmarked, which gladdened his heart, but also made his way on perilous—a matter of estimating degrees and times and speeds. As a precaution, he composed a letter to his fellow enthusiast, Dr. Fellows, and fixed it to his bundle of drawings and notes before packing them safely away:

Here, my esteemed friend and fellow enthusiast, and quite unexpectedly, I have at last made a real discovery! I believe this ruined city of Sidda to be indeed the cradle of civilization, a crude thing, but of immense scientific importance. It would seem to me that the courtyard walls—so immensely thick—were meant to support some further construction, since disappeared. From the evidence of the numerous wells, one can conjecture that this land was not always so dry, not always such a perfect desert as it is now. Many years before the birth of Christ, I think it quite reasonable to assume that some kind of trees may have grown here in reasonable abundance. Hence I conclude that the structure erected above these four walls was made of timber, and that has disappeared due to the action of the voracious ants and termites found in these parts. Projecting the angle of the walls skywards (see drawing numbered 14), you will see that we have a pyramidical edifice—not one such as is found in Egypt based on the equilateral triangle, but rather one that conforms exactly to the rule of isosceles. I have sketched out the possible method of construction for such a pyramid, using only short lengths of timber such as might have been available. It is my conviction that Sidda became subject to prolonged drought and was gradually abandoned. Some few of the inhabitants may well have taken the long route by sea to Egypt itself, and there, in the course of many years, refined their original structure.

This desert is an inhospitable place for any man and if by any chance, mishap should befall me in the course of my return to the capital I wish to entrust you, my esteemed friend, with the discovery of this inestimable treasure. I beg of you in the name of our long association and our common love of science to publish my findings as well as you can, and then make your way with all haste here to continue my work. I have no doubt but that items of immense value and beauty are to be found beneath the tombs.

Your affectionate friend, Carbourne.

NOT FORTY YEARS AGO, when the man standing before us today with a small ironic smile playing about his lips was still in the deep shade of his mother's womb—before we passed the millennium, before the shady dome was built— another guide, a short, fattish man not half so elegant, though just as perfectly spoken as ours, would have been much preoccupied with the story of Sidney Carbourne.

"It was only after Dr. Fellows' death," he says, "that this letter was found, plunging his family into disgrace. His daughter was so ashamed that she committed suicide. He had even passed off the drawings, which Carbourne had neglected to sign, as his own!"

There is more than a suspicion of military background about this other guide, and an angry passion about the eyes. His party, larger than ours, obeys his every instruction with alacrity: eyes right, eyes left, marching forth on the sand hot as coals. Yet they are freer than us in their dress: the women, hatless, in low-cut tops and calf-length dresses or baggy shorts, the men with blazers off, short-sleeved shirts undone at the neck and stained beneath the arms. Their skins are deeply tanned, even red and flaking here and there, but they do not care. They want to soak it all up, history and sunshine alike.

"I'm afraid the early history of archaeology is full of such unscrupulousness. These were colonial times. Foreigners came with their heads full of nonsense and everyone believed them." He laughs bitterly. Some of the party smile, but uncertainly—they are foreigners too and feel his contempt. "Nowadays we are much more scrupulous. Carbourne's theory, though correct in some respects, is largely a fairy tale fuelled by his consuming jealousy of a friend of his who had made his reputation and fortune by means of a discovery in Egypt. It was a minor one compared to what was to come, but considered important at the time. Sidney Carbourne dreamed of addressing the Royal Society back in England, but he never did. Some say that he wasn't even the first to discover Sidda: the remains of a single human skeleton of recent origin were found buried in a shallow grave.

"Carbourne's Pyramid is clearly a ridiculous hypothesis, easily disproved by a few calculations—" Forceful and intense, this other guide jabs contemptuously at the glass case containing Sidney's last written words, and a piece of pink stone he collected and marked with Indian ink. "In seeing Sidda merely as a precursor of Egyptian civilization he severely underestimated it. Nowadays," he stands a little straighter, "we value it as the first emergence of that ingenuity and fortitude we like to think of as an essential feature of our national character. Follow me!

"You have to imagine these surrounding lands, as Carbourne suggested, far greener than they are today. There was water in relative abundance, for beneath this sand is a thick band of rock and beneath that there were at the time underground streams. Here and there, a fault in the bed of rock allowed water to seep upwards, creating fertile patches of land. This area was particularly rich in such secret wells, and the Siddanese took a vital first step when they decided to dig down and search beneath the sand for the source of the damp. They found that as they went down the dampness increased, and that with much labour they could in the end tap the source of water itself. This was sufficient to turn them from a nomadic to a settled people. With the stones they had brought up from beneath the sand they began to build, and with the water they irrigated the land round about. By the second century of its existence Sidda had fifteen functioning wells. They can still be distinguished: the larger ones, clustered together to your left. Imagine how Sidda must have appeared to the traveller: a shimmering oasis of green on the horizon, scarcely believable in its beauty. As the land began to yield a surplus and trade developed, a class system began to emerge, with an upper tier of landowners and a lower of manual workers, employed year in year out with the cutting and carrying of stone and the transport of water. Above both of these were the four well guardians or priests, who ensured that life was lived so as to please the gods responsible for their city's good fortune. These four hexagonal towers were the priest houses. Follow me inside the courtyard!

"Imagine this sculpture in its full glory: beneath it was a powerful natural spring, forcing water upwards like a fountain. See how it's built from many stones, leaving cracks and fissures between which the water gushed out, then flowed down into the sand. If you will excuse the gesture—see how a little saliva brings out the rich green of the rock, so like the green of healthy leaves. This we think was the centre of the water ceremonies, in which celebrants approached from the four corners of the square along these paths, watched by the priests in their towers…"

Nowadays, this guide's story would not excite us. We'd know what was to come, and we'd turn away: "Then disaster struck!" Who wants to hear of such things? Who wants to see Mr. Melanoma's face? But back then it was different; they felt quite safe, and liked to hear of catastrophe.

"One by one the fifteen wells ran dry. Twenty-four new ones were dug in an increasingly desperate search for water, making the number up to thirty-nine. If you look at the path you're standing beside, you will see many fragments of pottery. Pick one up—you hold in your hand a pattern of lines and dots in which we can read the story of the end of Sidda. The marks are arranged in units ranging from fifteen to seventy-eight, which is twice thirty-nine. Each dot is a well still functioning, each line is a dry one. Thus we have a record of the fluctuating fortunes of the city, and indeed the main work of the Institute is now to arrange them chronologically so as to piece together a history of each well. Each fragment is part of a water bowl, and these, we think, were brought before the statue of the water god, filled, and then smashed on the way back out of the square as a gesture of homage and propitiation. Please put the pieces back.

"Gather around. I can show you here an exact replica from the last days—look: all lines. Empty, empty, empty. No water. Sidda was destroyed by the very forces of nature that had brought it into being in the first place, and its inhabitants were forced to take up again the harsh nomadic life of times before. Yet, naturally, we hope that one day the desert will flower again, and even now plans are afoot to bring a team of international scientists into the desert a little north of here in the hope of discovering underground waters. Then we could grow barley and tomatoes, avocado, watermelon, even strawberries, and you visitors would not see so many starving children begging in the street.

"Ladies and gentlemen, you will leave in ten minutes. Please ask me questions if you wish, or take a cold drink in the café by the car-park. Nowadays, I'm afraid the water is in bottles and comes many miles by road! Thank you." He salutes them at the end, looking over the tops of their heads at his imaginary oasis, of which there is now no trace.

"Where did you learn your English?" a woman with white skin baked brown but for the thin marks of swimsuit straps would have asked.

"In Oxford." He would have smiled. "I have read all your literature."

"What's your view of the dreadful bombings last week?" That would be the woman's husband, standing stiffly beside her. "I understand several tourists were killed."

"You must understand—" and then that other guide's face would have grown dark, "that we are struggling hard to establish ourselves as a nation in our own right, and no one is helping us. You might say we are trying to recreate, in hostile circumstances, a beautiful garden, such as once flourished here. Violence…such things are unpleasant, I think, but inevitable."

"Where would you be without tourism? It's crazy, blowing people up!" And a thin boy with very short hair would have asked, scratching at his scalp, red from the sun, "Where did the people live? Why aren't there any houses?"

"Because," that other guide would have declared, smiling again, "they were built of wood. And I expect you have seen the ants and termites in the grounds of your hotel? In two weeks one colony of termites can devour four tons of timber. The homes of the ancient Siddanese are nothing but dust blowing in the wind. Of course, now everything is painted with preservative."

WE CAN'T BLAME THESE other guides—times change—nor must we forget them: they are part of the picture too.

"But," says our guide now, and I feel as if behind those thick, dark lenses he is staring straight at me, "they were telling—if we are charitable—half-truths. Sidda is the most misunderstood archaeological site on the face of the earth. Today, I will tell you facts.

"How many people do you think occupied this site? Five hundred? A thousand? The answer is none. *City* isn't really the appropriate term for Sidda. We think of cities as bustling centres of trade, places on a crossroads where people gather and live in close proximity. Sidda was indeed a busy place, but no one lived here. It was the creation of many people who lived scattered about in the surrounding lands, but it was not their home.

"It was one of the fundamental beliefs of the ancient Siddanese that *individuals* should leave nothing behind them. When a house fell into disuse, such materials as could not be reused were burned and the ashes scattered to the winds. And when a person died, their body was taken to a lonely place and left unguarded on the sand so that ants and vultures could feast upon the flesh. A year later, the bones were buried, without marking, deep in the desert sand. This way, please…"

A trickle of sweat runs down between my shoulder blades, and somehow sand has slipped inside my shoes: I can feel the tiny grains pressing in. We gather quietly around our guide without him having to ask and wait for the two old ones to catch up, inching forward on the uneven ground.

"The only memorial allowed the dead can in fact be seen right at your feet: these countless pottery shards, which are all fragments of decorated bowls, some large, some small. The day of the bowl came after the day of the bones, and on it the dead person's relatives carried his or her drinking bowl to the city of Sidda and once within the confines of the city"—he holds up an imaginary bowl, then brings his hands suddenly down—"smashed it on the ground. Every night the day's shards were swept into the four sunken paths, gradually filling them, until, as you can see, they are almost level with the rest of the ground."

The pottery fragments are dry, reddish and open-pored. As people shift on their feet I can hear them crunch and snap.

"But Sidda isn't simply a city of remembrance. It's also a monument. Two contradictory impulses were behind its painstaking creation: On the one hand a desire to honour the Siddanese way of life—obsession might be a better word, for it was long before they were in any danger of extinction that building commenced, and on the other, the urge to hide it from other peoples' understanding and, in particular, that of those coming after them. Sidda was built to impress, but not to inform. And largely, until now, it has succeeded." He beckons; we draw more closely around and watch him reach into his pocket.

"Consider the alphabet. Here are examples of some of the commonest symbols. They consist of collections of dots and lines, up to thirty-nine of each per unit, which can be enclosed in a circle or a rectangle and arranged either horizontally or vertically in various orders. This is not a picture alphabet, but a phonetic one. Each unit represents a sound. A rectangle or a circular enclosure implies a stressed or unstressed sound—syllable is not the correct term, for the language of Sidda was composed literally of strings of sounds, each discrete. Now, please pass these around…"

The piece I hold is roughly triangular, but slightly curved. The inside is smooth, and a slightly darker red. I turn it over: there they are, the ridges and the dots, carefully traced, perhaps with a twig.

"Close your eyes," our guide says, "and touch it lightly with your fingertips…Yes. Can you feel the difference between the bumps and the holes? The ridges and the lines? I think you'll find that if you run your fingernail across, it's quite easy to count them rapidly." We do so. The sound, like the buzz of tiny crickets, is all around me and continues as he speaks.

"You understand? This is an alphabet of the blind. But not, like our Braille, a second-hand thing, representing another alphabet, representing in turn a language spoken and invented by the sighted, that is, an alphabet *for* not *of* the blind. No. This alphabet represents a language created and spoken by the sightless, and the city around you was built entirely by a race of people who could not see." I open my eyes briefly, am dazzled by the light, close them again.

"There are several theories. My colleague, Professor Nielsen, has recently published his theory that the Siddanese blinded their own offspring at birth, much as in some cultures the foreskin is automatically removed. And I believe Mossinsky has argued that the Siddanese were in fact a community of outcasts from the surrounding regions, where it is well known that many tribes expelled those with mental or physical abnormalities. The sight-less, he argues, continued this custom in their own way by keeping themselves apart and developing a culture so arcane as to be impenetrable to the other groups and the tribes that had expelled them. Intriguing as both these hypotheses are, they do in the end seem over-elaborate to me. It seems far more likely that these people were, like myself, born sightless—" Everyone opens their eyes wide at this. "Or else victims of a progressive dulling of their sight due to genetically inherited disease, or the fearful intensity of the desert light." One and all we stare at our elegant guide, peer at his close-fitting glasses, so very dark. Is he really telling the truth? But we don't dare ask, and anyway, he reads our minds.

"Indeed. I find my way around this city by memory, the feel of the ground under my feet, my sense of where shadows fall—and something more than any of these—a feeling that I have always known the city of Sidda. Outside I carry a stick, but here it has never seemed necessary.

"To return to the alphabet. Whilst it has so far been impossible to decode more than a handful of words, we have learned the way in which it was written: not left to right, right to left or up and down, but starting always with the first symbol enclosed in a square centrally positioned in the available space. The next would be to the top left corner, top right corner, bottom right, bottom left; those following would be positioned between the top right of the outer top left symbol and the top left of the outer top right symbol and so on, forming a regular pattern like checks— or a honeycomb—of symbols and space. We think, for instance, that these symbols make up the word for *her* or *his*, and these make up the word for bowl. Perhaps this one is bone. Of course, we have no idea as to which sound a given letter represents. It's my view the alphabet will never be fully understood."

Mr. Melanoma holds his piece of pottery out to give it back. I slip mine in my bag: it'll do no harm, I think. There are plenty more.

The thick pink walls cut off our view of the desert; the path that snaps like brittle bones beneath our feet leads straight as a die to the sculpture where Sidney Carbourne tied his camel.

"It's the only pictorial image of any kind the Siddanese left in their city," our guide says. "The stone is of uniform colour, but see how the texture varies"—he reaches out— "here porous, here almost as smooth as glass, with the smoothest pieces of all used for the face and arms. Note the intricacy of the work on the face: no less than forty pieces, carefully chosen to indicate the ears, nose and mouth. The space beneath the brows is blank—and what other reason could there be for this than that the Siddanese knew how they differed from others? This sculpture could rank alongside any of the great pieces in the world, above them all, I say, for consider how it was made without sight and without tools, other than perhaps another stone to knock a corner off here and there: what judgment and patience, what philosophy, must have gone into its construction!

"Around this statue, ladies and gentlemen, the Siddanese gathered to produce and appreciate their culture. They travelled many miles from their flimsy homes, going always on foot. They sang and played instruments, they told stories and riddles, and drank an intoxicant brewed from moulds cultivated inside the mouths of the thirty-nine pits beyond the square. Traces of this mould have been found on the concave surfaces of the pottery fragments we have discussed, and inside the hexagonal towers which we deduce to be public kitchens. Under the influence of this drink, they became convinced that they could read the future. They saw or guessed how their own demise would come, and how the sighted world would inevitably misunderstand their achievements. Consider these people, blind, scattered, knowing themselves to be unique in their peaceful and economical culture: proud, and justifiably so, but also vulnerable, afraid and alone. Perhaps it's not surprising that they wanted to build a city such as this, itself a riddle that could be unlocked only by the knowing touch of those, like them, free of the distraction of sight.

"Ladies and gentlemen, you have here a moving testimony as to the diversity of our species. For almost two thousand years the Siddanese lived here, in a completely different manner from the other peoples of the world. Navigating in their inner darkness across the desert, they built a city without the use of tools; they refrained from eating meat or using animals as beasts of burden, they avoided trade and eschewed science: developing not astronomy like the Egyptians nor geometry like the Greeks but their own austere metaphysics and philosophy. Whilst all the other peoples of the globe were slaves to superstition, the Siddanese pondered the problems of communication and interpretation, fitting one stone carefully on top of the next. Whilst others looked back to the origins of the gods and sought to bend nature to their own will, the Siddanese felt their way forward to the future and guessed what was to come. But as well as all this, I like to think of them as a deeply sensual as well as a serious people, rather as I like to see myself." He smiles at us properly for the first time.

"We are lucky, I think, that such a people lived. You may take photographs if you wish, though remember, this place is not designed to appeal to the eyes! There are various publications on sale by the entrance, and some small-scale replicas of the statue: an intriguing puzzle which you can try to assemble yourselves. I suggest that in the few remaining minutes you close your eyes and explore Sidda by touch, for it's only in darkness that its full beauty can be appreciated."

Nowadays no one asks questions of a guide. It either works or it does not. He moves to wait in the shade for the next group. Gratefully, I close my eyes again and wander, arms outstretched, blundering unpractised until my fingers touch Sidda's walls. I feel the sun's fatal heat on my back as I trace the border between one stone and the next. I slip my fingernail into the gap between. I feel how in these last hot days and years the world is full of parables, prefiguration and correspondence. Even half-truths or outright lies hide lessons and examples, and somewhere, beneath one of these dry stones, curled like a bug, is hope. I can hear other people on the path, and the cry of the veiled woman's child, but apart from that it is quiet under the dome. I press against the wall, opening myself to its roughness and accumulated warmth. I have come to my last site. I want to touch our guide, to take his hand in mine—it would be dry and warm, like the stone—with my eyes still closed.

I know that there may be yet other guides. I know that they may even come in shapes different than ours—limbless, green-skinned, minute, extra-sensory, photosynthetic, mechanic, invisible: "We're nearing the end of our tour. Just one more thing—below is the planet earth. Mostly desert now, though once it was uniquely fertile and inhabited by many forms of life, one of which came to dominate, and, we guess, was responsible for the change. We're passing now over one of the smaller sites they occupied: you can see the form of a circle, and inside that a square, with several smaller circles scattered about. These beings left their mark, but they had no culture to speak of, and have often been compared, in their compulsion to build and multiply without thought, to the blue beetles which caused such havoc on our planet some years ago."

"But on what evidence do we make such statements about their culture?" says one of these beings, maybe not through lips and teeth with air, but somehow, somehow. "No one's troubled to go and look, have they?" Already it's gone, passed from view; but the shape of Sidda and the idea of those earth-beetles long ago move her, and she decides she will return one day to vindicate their name...

That's hope! I walk slowly beside the wall, just grazing it with my fingertips. I sense where it ends just before my fingers slip into air. And I believe the blind man who waits in the shade; I must. I have closed my eyes and touched one of the wonders of the world, forgotten for a moment the terrible heat and the fearful sound of a wind blowing full of sand.

Low Tide

I T WAS HOT, the sky a bowl of blue; waves slapped against the rock. I remember still the astounding sensation of the air on my face, stomach, shoulders, back and limbs—all over, like invisible hands. How it was to stand upright on new legs and feet: utterly strange, yet easy, and then, a moment later, such a feeling of weight! The land's pull made each step an intentional thing and turned mere standing into an act of resistance. Intensely aware of my new flesh, I waded ashore and walked along the beach, leaving my prints in damp, newly exposed sand: my heels, the balls of my feet, my ten toes.

At the far end of the bay was a small island and a white and red lighthouse. A rowboat had been dragged up on the beach and by the boat stood a man, watching me through binoculars. Did his watching change me that first time? Or did I, wet-dreaming until I caught fire, invent him, then split my pelt with longing and climb out of it? Maybe it was both of these things; in any case, at the beginning neither of us cared. When I drew closer, I noticed his clothes: long pants, a shirt, a jacket, all of them faded by the sun and ruffled by the breeze. Thinking that I might yet need my old sleek skin I looked back then to the rocks, but the tide had turned and they were all but submerged. For a moment then I felt the sharpness of the sand blown in the breeze, and knew that the sun could burn me. And I missed my kind, the underwater sounds, all the old freedoms, but I told myself: *No matter, you must go on now*, and walked towards the man, who let the binoculars hang about his neck and strode, then ran to meet me.

His beard and hair were a mid brown, wiry, trimmed, if roughly so. I liked his face. It broke open and contradicted itself: he smiled, yet his cheeks were wet, his eyes, sea-green, wide with astonishment.

"I knew you must come back!" He gasped for breath, his hands heavy on my shoulders. "But not like this! Where the hell are your clothes?" He laughed, sloughed his jacket, held it out for me, though I did not feel embarrassed, despite the way his gaze exposed me even as I covered myself. I noticed his skin glistened with sweat. Would mine do the same?

"I've come from the sea," I told him, "I left my coat on the rock." My voice emerged rough-edged, sore. He raised the binoculars again. "I think I see something dark in the water. We'll take the boat and look."

So we pushed out. He took the oars and I the glasses, and I quickly learned how to use them to bring the distance close. At times I too thought I could see a dark thing floating just below the surface of the water, but once we drew close I understood that it was nothing but a reflection of the rock, and despite him saying that whatever I had left there would likely wash up on the shore, I knew that I must act as if my old skin was gone, and that now I must live on land.

He said he was my *husband*. He kept the lighthouse, and as well as that, he was a kind of artist, one who used science in the service of beauty, he said. Surely I remembered that? And the bed he had built for us on the third floor of the tower? Our wedding day, the drunken priest? The night of the storm?

"I remember none of it," I told him. I was sitting on a pile of sacks in the stern of the boat. The ocean was flat and glossy, as the tide flowed in and bit by bit filled up the bay it rippled gently as if there were muscles beneath its skin. Reflected light flickered on our faces. The man who claimed to have married me looked away a moment, then back.

"That may be for the best," he said. "Everything will be better this time, Marina, I promise you. I'm very sorry. I think I had every right to be angry, but I never meant to hurt you."

Naturally, I marked the word, *hurt*. And yet I knew that it was not me that he spoke of, and he seemed sincere. I liked his smoothness, the lean, muscular look of him, his strong-fingered hands, the intensity of his gaze. And that first time, constrained as we were by oars shelved to each side of us and by the struts and seats but most of all by being in a small vessel floating on the roof of my former world, can only be called exquisite: sex so gentle in its beginnings, so constrained and restrained—yet only seeming so, for within those limits our bodies' sensations were amplified like voices trapped in a cave, and at the end, shuddering, we broke free of all bounds, left the world and returned to it as if new. I saw, afterwards, that his hand bled from where he had slipped it between me and the floor of the boat.

MARINA, HE CALLED ME, yet he never thought to introduce himself and I discovered his name only after he had taught me to read. From the start, he taught me a great deal. That first day he showed me how to manage the oars and it was I who pulled us back to the lighthouse island, along the narrow cove to the one place where it was possible, at certain times of day, to land. Together we hauled the boat beyond the tide mark and secured it with rocks. "You can walk around the island in an hour," he told me. By then, he had stopped saying that surely I remembered, and simply explained how things were and would be, though he frequently grasped my hand, as if to be sure that I was real.

He showed me a vegetable garden, a garden shed, a chicken coop, a smoke hut. The keeper's cottage, low with thick walls and small windows, was built right up against the tower. A smaller dwelling closer to the garden stood empty: out of parsimony, he said, the Lighthouse Board had not yet replaced the deputy keeper. His face darkened and he added that it was all the same to him, and likely they never would…"In any case," he told me, gesturing at the tower, "the deputy is an unnecessary position now that my gearing system has so much improved the efficiency of the clockwork. The winding schedule is very manageable. You'll see."

In the future, he told me, all lighthouses would be powered by electricity, a thing like lightning, controlled. And they would be connected by another system of wires that carried voices from place to place and even from one continent to another…But the very remotest of them, such as East Point, would likely wait until last. "And so until then," he said, pushing open the door into the kitchen, which was shady now but still warm from the range on the far wall, "we'll live here and be the world to each other." He pulled me close and reached under the jacket to feel the slippery heat between my legs. His hands shook as he unfastened the horn buttons, and soon we made good use of the table.

How willing I was! He liked that. Likewise, I told him, and he liked that too. Both of us were greedy for pleasure. But more than that, I craved the deep forgetting at the heart of the act of love, that shedding of the trivial particulars that separate one being, one species, from another. Our desires were attuned, our bodies spoke. He fitted me. I liked him well, from the length and firmness of what he called his member to the gleam of his body hair in the firelight and the long muscles of his arms and legs. He seemed a good mate, even though after the act he must ask, whispering, his lips to my ear, his hands restless on my skin,

"Did you open yourself like this to *him*? Even if you did so, I do forgive you, because you have returned. But tell me, please."

"I don't understand," I said and pulled away.

AFTERWARDS I WAS ALWAYS raging hungry, but I knew nothing of cooking and kitchens. This too I learned, though only to a degree: I kept my taste for raw things, and ours was a poor diet apart from the fish, mussels, and eggs. We had carrots, potatoes, cabbage and dill. Flour-and-water biscuits. Bitter coffee. Dried beans to be soaked in the pot. Ham. Salted butter and even saltier meats in cans. We frequently needed some brandy to wash down our meal.

And neither could I sew, and I saw no reason to. The machinery of the light interested me more. Above us, burning always, was the enormous light, reached by a long spiral climb that felt to me as if I was ascending inside a giant shell. The four oil lamps at the top of the tower were set inside a first order Fresnel lens taller than a man, a glass beehive, he called it, though also, I thought, it could be an gigantic insect eye. In daytime, the lens glittered and took on the colours of the sea and sky; at night its many planes glowed, so that it appeared to hover in the room: a hallucinatory vessel, a ship that might have travelled from beyond the moon. There were eight bullseyes to magnify the light. Above and below each of these were the panels set with many glass pieces. Each of these nine hundred and forty-four curved sections had been individually cut and ground and then set exact in its curved brass mount. Light, like the sea, was made of waves, he said, and these glass prisms caught and focussed waves into a narrow, concentrated beam that could be seen twenty miles out to sea. Floating on mercury and driven by elaborate clockwork, the lamps revolved inside the lens, giving the beam its characteristic pulse.

Despite the ceiling ventilation it was unbearably hot near the light. Below, in the watch room it was cooler, and there, at five in the morning and five in the afternoon, without fail, we re-filled the kerosene, and wound the clockwork tight. It was a circular room, with strong oak floors to support all our supplies and equipment, and generous windows all around to let in light. There was a desk, where the lighthouse records were written, and shelves where they were kept; a narrow door led out to the observation platform. The platform was also used to support the ladder when the light room windows were cleaned after heavy storms, and in any case, according to regulation, no less than four times a year. Also in the watch room was a bed built out from the wall: Why, he said, add in a journey up and down the spiral stairs when night observations needed to be taken? And why be separated? Why stay down in the gloom of the cottage, when there was so much light to be had and we could see each other so very well?

"I shouldn't believe in you," he said, looking up into my face while I knelt astride him on that bed, rocking, squeezing just enough to keep us both on the brink of our double descent, "but I must."

I ALWAYS BELIEVED IN HIM. But at night my underwater dreams seemed just as true: the dives and twists, the impossible grace and freedom of a lost world. More than once I woke in tears and the feeling lasted for days: a terrible grief and longing to be where I could no longer survive. All I could do then was gaze out to sea, or walk the shore cursing myself for being careless; I yearned for that dense, oily fur, the fat-sheathed musculature beneath. There was no remedy. But if he was gentle, he could ease me back to the pleasures of our life on the island off East Point, where gulls and terns and albatrosses soared and wheeled and plummeted into the water, and the wind blew clean and constant, bending the low grasses and the wildflowers and the few small trees back towards the mainland, and bringing with it the smells of ozone and kelp and emptiness, while all the time the clouds it pushed across the sky stretched and grew and shrank and grew again.

Still surrounded by the sea, I lived on land, a wife of sorts. I practised my letters. I learned how to keep the record. In a single sentence, that ran across the width of the book, I must include the weather, any passing vessels, any incidents, and the state of the equipment and supplies. I learned about the winds and Mr. Howard's names for the clouds: the veils of cirrostratus, the ominous mounds of cumulonimbus, heavy with rain. I learned how to trim the lamps and clean the parts of lens, how to use the telescope, how to calculate distance, read a chart and judge the course of a ship.

He did explain the camera, yet would not teach me to use it: the apparatus and the process were still in development, he said, the chemicals noxious…More than that, I think, its power was new and excited him to a point that he could not bear to share it. He believed the camera would eventually be able to capture even the subtlest effects of the weather on the sea, and motion itself, but for now, the subject must remain still for minutes on end while the light worked its transformation on the plate. He could not have enough portraits: I posed both with and without clothes, standing, sitting and lolling on the rocks, in the water walking the beach, on the bed; I posed even while I slept, and was later able to see how soft and peaceful my face appeared when my eyes were closed.

HE HAD A CHEST OF CLOTHING which he said was mine. *All right!* A woman's, at least, he said. Though why? I was comfortable enough in his shirts.

"Just try them," he said. "I want to see." We rifled through and I marvelled at the vast skirts, a boned bodice, at the tiny mother-of-pearl buttons on the placket and sleeves of elaborate shirts patterned with tiny flowers and needle-fine stripes. Everything but the skirts and bloomers looked too small. But the rustle of it all! Such stuff! I tied the corset around my head with a shirt, pulled a pair of drawers over his.

"Like this?"

"Though of course," he said once our laughter subsided, "this is what you will have to wear when Mr. Davis visits to make the inspection at the end of the month."

"Really?" I told him, wiping my eyes. "You'll have to show me how."

He reached into the chest and pulled out two small shapeless pieces of fabric.

"For your legs," he explained. "Would you please just try them?"

The material, I later learned, was made from moth cocoons and the finest, water-repellent wool of a special breed of sheep; all clothes then were made from beasts and plants. And the stockings did settle lightly on my skin, almost but not quite as if they were part of me. Serious, then, he fetched his camera, set up the stand, then posed me on the bed all but nude, propped up on my elbows, legs akimbo, in such a way that any viewer's gaze would follow the dark lines of my stockinged legs to where my sex, part anemone, part oyster, stretched between the two white strips of upper thigh.

"Don't blink. Stay still," he warned me, the watch ticking in his hand.

And after that, there were yet more photographs. These light pictures, he told me, made by and of the real body, were no mere daubs or imitations or interpretations, but a physical print of sex itself—that raw thing which joined humankind to the beasts, the irrational heart in the thinking machine, the greedy void that hid beneath the skirts of romance, the thing that lodged not just between our legs but also somewhere deep in the brain, hidden in a place which would some day be found and understood…The century to come, he told me, would be all about seeing the invisible, the interiors of our bodies and minds, the atoms of matter, the surfaces of the moon and stars. Open your legs wider, he said. Touch yourself.

And after all, he decided, it was far better that the inspector did not see me. Let alone the challenge of dressing—her things, whoever she was, did not fit me, a woman still part wild—his neglect in reporting my return would involve too much explanation. The smokehouse was the obvious place for me to hide during the inspection. But it was always possible that just this once Mr. Davis would decide to glance in there, or that I might grow restless, peer out of the window as they passed and give us both away...Did I understand how important discretion was?

Not really, no. Not yet. Any suspicions I had floated too deep to see or really feel; I knew only that something new burned inside him and I did not like it.

Suppose I waited the visit out in the bay at the north end? The inspector would never go there, would not even know such a private spot existed. Or better still, leave me on the mainland—I'd shelter in a cave or bush until it was safe to return...I do believe the keeper saw the sense of these stratagems, and even wanted to enact them. But he could not. He could not allow me to be beyond his sight and reach.

"Why ask," I said, "if you will not hear what I say?" He caught me by the arm as I turned away; I bit him, drew blood. We fought hard, breathed in grunts as we yanked and twisted, gasping at what the other could inflict, though either we were perfectly matched or neither of us was quite prepared to deliver defeat; our struggle took us to the ground, and there turned blow by blow into its opposite, or else love became a battle; it's hard to say which, and when we woke, bruised and aching in the half-light of a new morning we were shocked at ourselves, terrified, when we realized that we had slept, fucked or fought through changing of the lamps. A strong wind buffeted the tower and though there was no sign of any harm done, we might never know if someone had been misled by the darkness, whether we had done any harm.

We were both overwrought, he said, and offered a tonic: another of his inventions. Just a few drops on the tongue—a sweetness, which soon became metallic. Then a vast, dense fog surrounded and infiltrated me, overwhelmed all my senses; sight, then hearing, touch and smell. I slept so soundly that I could neither move nor cough, but for good measure he tied me and fit me inside a box: I know this only because of the photograph. And shortly after I came to in the watch room, weak, hungry and at the same time nauseated, the birth pangs began to roll through my lower belly and up the insides of my thighs.

He would not seek help. There *was* none, he said.

Limbless, covered in thick fur, her small face arranged around dark, deep eyes like mine, our child was stillborn. I wrapped her and held her close, knew I must return her to the sea and begged him to let me go down to the rocks. "I'll take you," he said, and though his voice was gentle, he was rightly fearful that I might swim away or drown myself. He grasped my hand tight and would not let go as we clambered back from the water's edge.

And perhaps it was to the good, he said, adding syrup and a measure of brandy into hot tea: the same for each of us, and I watched him drink first. The island was no place for a child, he said. Mere breeding was not what free thinkers such as he and I were for.

Free?

He said that he understood that I was sad, that words failed me, but he knew it would pass. And luckily, we had our work for the light, the routine around which all else must be fitted…Winter would come soon, bringing storms. We must eat well, gather back our strength, and put everything in order.

Now he wore the keys at his waist and locked doors behind him. When he was away, I was bound to the bed. And yet I also worked my share, cleaning the panels of the lens, and, when permitted on the windy platform outside the watch room, I scanned the sea for ships. I explored my prison too; I found, folded and tucked into the back of the Bible an article headlined *Tragic Death at East Point*: Two days after the storm of November 3rd, the battered body of the deputy lightkeeper at East Point had been found washed up some three miles south of the island, following a failed attempt to launch the lightship craft in order to aid a whaler in distress. The fate of the whaler was still unknown.

A small key at the back of the desk drawer led me to a box containing a single photographic print of a woman who could only be my namesake: she wore the clothes I had handled, and stood against the whitewashed cottage wall, her blonde hair blurring in the breeze. Beneath the photograph was a lock of red-gold hair, and a copy of the signed statement the keeper had submitted the day following the discovery of his colleague's body. *I was sadly mistaken*, he wrote, *in thinking my poor wife cured of an infirmity for which she had in the past been treated. Acting impulsively during a fit of hysterical mania brought on by the storm and feelings of guilt concerning the loss of the deputy, she cast herself into the water while I slept.*

AND NOW THE DAYS SHORTENED; flocks of birds passed, returning north across the vastness of the ocean. I said nothing to the keeper, but thought often of Marina, whose body had never been found. Had she loved the deputy keeper, or simply been the object of his affections? I did not like to think of her as drowned, let alone murdered. Did she go into the sea? Perhaps she was like me, but able to return? Had she found her skin? Or did she swim in the awkward human way to the mainland, and make some kind of escape…Who knew, I told myself, but that she might be living with natives in the bush, or have got so far as the town and have booked her passage out under a new name. Out there on the platform, buffeted by the winds, I breathed in the cold salt air and watched the seabirds, marvelling at the way they stayed together, and at the steady beating of their wings, mile on mile. The largest birds, the mollymawks, pass without apparent movement or effort through the air; their wings fixed, just barely tilting from side to side to ride the currents like waves, they simply turn their heads the way they wish to go…Such huge birds, the mollies, yet it was as if they had no weight. I watched them slip and soar and it lifted my heart. I longed for the bird-feeling and imagined it: the ocean and the land spread out beneath in intricate detail, but also in depth and with extraordinary focus. In my mind's eye I saw as if from very far above the rocks the island and the tower where I myself stood looking out. The wind blew steadily to the east and the air seemed to offer itself to me. And I would not go back inside, would not endure another night with Clarence Morgan, the clockwork beneath us unwinding itself cog by cog until the next time it must be set, and the next, and the next. Ignoring his call, I climbed onto the rails, balanced for one terror-stricken moment then gave myself to the wind. Immediately I felt the new strength in my chest and back, the structural dominance of two great limbs.

The water below was almost pink. Just two wing-beats, and I was rising fast. I could no longer hear his call, and did not look back, for the air is a kind of ecstasy, a far freer thing than even a swimmer could believe.

Yet I'll admit that come spring, on my way to the grounds, I did return, and landed on a low cliff to watch my former keeper, on the beach below, set up a new version of his camera. The apparatus was directed at the seals sunning themselves on the rocks. He was thinner and older than I recalled. He had broken his promise not to hurt me, and there was a gun slung over his shoulder which I knew he might use. Yet even so, watching him, I felt for the first time the need to open my wings wide and stretch my neck to its utmost, then tuck my head deep down this way, then that, to stretch and bow and tread out the steps of our dance. A sound came out of me, part shriek, part moan: oh, look at me! For looking is the beginning of the dance. He must see me exactly as I am and what I do, the exact way of it, and I, likewise. And by scrupulous imitation, turn on turn, we come to see better and prove to each other that we see, and what we see. We must show that each can and will exactly follow the other, or, failing, try again...

Hearing me, the keeper turns and reaches for his binoculars. He faces me, but gives no sign of recognition or sympathy. My call dies in my throat; I put myself into the wind, run, and scull hard until the updraft bears me and I ride suddenly without effort and free of the earth's jealous pull; I soar above vast ocean into the even vaster air. I must fly on to the place where I will meet my kind, and find the one with whom I can perfect the dance.

My Beautiful Wife

THIS, HERE, IS THE BEGINNING of spring: the snow has melted; it is a yellow-grey day, and faintly raining. Gulls tear the still air with their screams, wheel between the concrete blocks, settle on the chimneys and on the mud-green balconies and their empty flower troughs. And now for the first time in many months the tape has been peeled off, the catches oiled, the double glazed panes pulled in: the windows are flung open to be cleaned. Siiri Nistsoo shakes her rug from her balcony. My neighbours pause at the doorways to the staircases and talk. Perhaps they seem to stand straighter than last week; certainly the courtyard paths have reappeared now that the snow is gone and children play on the red climbing frame by the stand of birch trees; they spatter themselves with mud and the last of the slush as they rush from the bottom of the slide to the steps at the back. Two of my neighbours' wives, both hatless for the first time this year and wearing the self-same purple anorak from Lauduhama, watch over them with half an eye, while Ralf Jarlik, once an engineer, now a member of the parliament, crosses from 134 House to empty his rubbish bucket into the skips that stand in the middle of the courtyard. He's wearing a good coat these days. A scrawny Alsatian sniffs at the mud. The gulls caw and wheel, caw and wheel. Television aerials stretch from the flat roofs, quiver, point in the direction of news: there is more of it now, and more reliable.

Soon, Liia said this morning, we will be able to wear our summer clothes. All these small changes are important.

For example, because it is the weekend, Liia makes proper coffee, from beans, which last year were unavailable. The quality could still be better, but even so we savour its complex bitterness as our eyes rove through the window— out, always out. The place would look less anonymous, I think, if the windows and balconies of each block were painted a different colour. I tell Liia I might suggest it: little improvements are happening all the time. But really they should blow the whole district up and start again. If it could be afforded.

At least, says Liia (she always tries to make things bearable) there are trees within sight of the windows, on one side. But the kitchen is too small, as the English say, to swing a cat in. It always has been so, but I find it seems even smaller now. The sink on its brackets, not level, a row of the green swirled tiles behind it. The folding table, the round topped plywood stools pushed under it, the two shelves: everyone has them. The cooker, once white enamel, its lid that no longer folds down, its leak that no one could ever

78

fix. How sick of it I am. We are lucky to have no children and so enjoy three other rooms—a study each and a bedroom which we also use as a lounge. We need all that space for our books.

Yesterday, my wife Liia said to me: "Tell me, Toomis, why is it that I can never-ever find a book in this collection of ours?" She stood at the threshold between our two studies. Her white-gold hair was just brushed and bristled with electricity. She wears it cut simply, straight, at shoulder length with a fringe. She has scarcely aged in fifteen years. Her voice, I thought, was teasing.

"I don't know, my love, my little berry," I told her, "but what is it you want? I will find it for you." The library system is perfectly workable. Chronology is the most important factor, but here and there I think an author deserves to have all his works next to each other, however long he lived. And then again sometimes a volume on the history of France makes connections with one from Political Theory or English Literature and so I might put the two of them together. Then of course, I put those I use most nearest to my desk, which can only be sensible. I have explained this before, but she will not agree.

"You are just like a man," she said. Of course I am! But that, she said, is not what she means. She went back into her own study. She is a translator, I am a historian (though I have worked mainly as a language teacher and currently am of necessity in a clerical role: perhaps that explains this disagreement over the library system).

And then mischief entered me. Just like a man, I thought. What a statement! I went from shelf to shelf, pulling out books. The yellow books and then the red and the blue, the white spines and the brown. It took an hour or so, extracting them from their correct places, deciding where to draw the line between orange and red, and which colours to put next to each other. I dusted them and ranked them, by hue, on a single shelf. It cheered me up, as physical work can, so I started to whistle, and the sound of that brought her in.

"What's this?" she said.

"Is this a woman's system then?" I asked. "Will this suit you?" I found myself laughing like a schoolboy, uncontrollable; I did not understand why I was doing it. I am not a frivolous person, I thought, even as I continued to laugh and she stared gravely at me. Eventually, she smiled and only then I stopped. Oh, she said, but how long did it take you to do this, my love? Do we have so much time to spare? It was a joke, I told her, only that. But somehow it was not the truth.

There are cars now, parked in a neat row at the edge of the green. All sorts of people have them. What use is a car, Liia says. Books are more important. A car can only take you half as far as the fuel you can pay for lasts, and then you have to come back; but books are infinite journeys and each one can be taken many times. We two, she smiles, are old travellers, *n'est ce pas*?

I was her teacher once, and she the cleverest student I ever had. And I was married to someone else, but I left, because not to would have been unbearable. In books, we renewed our passion, secretly at first, then frankly. We met other worlds and then returned to each other. Much of the past twenty years Liia and I have spent reading.

Back then, what we read rarely had consequences. The ideas could not grow. They came from elsewhere, like seeds blown on the wind, and depended on freedom's climate to grow: that was why we loved them so. I realize now that when I imagined the revolution, before it happened, I thought of it in terms of what we would be able to read. I thought of reading works by people who were only reputations to me, magic names, pregnant with many possibilities, of finding books I had hunted for in vain; they would fall into my hands like ripe plums. I dreamed of owning my own copy of an important text, being able to write pencilled notes on the page. I imagined gifts of books between me and my wife and the conversations we would have about them; I thought of books in our own language as well as foreign ones. That was what excited me about freedom. Since it has happened, I see of course that it means other things as well, instead, even. Perhaps the thing is that before we had only books? Somehow, I cannot read today.

The spring disturbs me. It is a time of longing. Paths criss-cross the courtyard, leading to other blocks like this and other courtyards and eventually to the woods, where the march bells will soon be out, then the crocuses and daffodils. We will go as soon as the mud has dried. Oh, summer…At this point, we all long for it, for the trees, the myriad rustlings and the light through leaves, for the long days, the feeling of sun on our skins, the other pleasure of shade. Picnics. I would like to have a car.

But that is the future still. Now, the rain begins to fall more heavily. One day in this country, I often say, we will learn to make drains, which currently exist only in the dictionary. One day, Liia said to me yesterday, we will learn how to talk to each other in different ways. Which way? How, different?

In the afternoon, I take the trolleybus to the market. My wife used to do this but some time back she said that she goes three times in the week and why should it not be shared? And I said that I am both working and studying at night school and so have less time, but, she said, who makes you do that? So I go to please her. At the entrance a row of people stand with puppies huddled in their coats or sleeping in straw shopping bags, all newness, shining fur, half-human faces, clean paws.

I go past the tools and vacuum parts, the military paraphernalia which only tourists buy. On through the new clothes, stall after stall, garments I don't even recognize, colours I don't have names for. Past the imported groceries tied to the shelves with string, the fat overwintered carrots in their dirt, the new potatoes, the churns of milk, the apples in piles. There are bananas everywhere now, but still too expensive for regular use. I buy sausage, bottled peas, bread and a chicken. Old women stash their money away in broken purses, kept among the cuts of meat. There is never enough change! A plastic bag costs thirty cents. It takes longer than you might think. All these things, the quantities, the choices, it is tiring somehow.

When I get back, there is a small pile of books on the rug in the centre of my room. The door to her study is ajar.

What is this? I call. Those: they are the books written by women, she calls back. I am sure that she is wrong, and look for myself, but I only find two more.

But what do you mean by it? I ask, standing at the threshold of her room. She pauses in her typing but doesn't turn her head. A good book is a good book, I say, surely, whoever has written it? I'm not sure, she says, it's just that I never thought to do it before. Simply to count. She laughs. Then she looks at me and I can't name the expression. Somewhere between shy and amazed.

Something must have made you think of it, I say. This is the twentieth century and she is no longer translating just the classics, but contemporary works also. Yes, she says, I wonder: would I ever have thought of it on my own? She's talking to herself. For a second, I feel invisible.

Currently, at the office, I am compiling biographies of our politicians. There is to be a brochure, issued to everyone in the country, detailing their professions, family status, and beliefs as well as a symbol for the party they stand for and a photograph. And at night, I read about economics and make summaries—this is for my Diploma in International Relations: it is no use being only a historian. Neither is it much use, in my opinion, having a government of poets forever. Besides, if they stop writing we will have no literature!

We need a new kind of politician, I tell Liia over supper. She has forgotten to take off her reading glasses and they steam up in the heat of the soup. The ingredients are much better now. We can savour what we eat, make it last with talk as they do in Europe, in novels. Yes, I say, we need a new kind of man, one who has an overview, and not served under previous conditions of course, because old habits—not so much of thought but of behaviour—die hard. I study her as I speak.

My wife is a very elegant woman. The cloth we have here is not of the best quality, but she wears the things she has made as if they were couture. She is slender, her hair the colour of winter sunlight, her skin, though it suffers a little at this time of year, is smooth as the finest paper. Her grey-green eyes call to mind the sea, the flecks of gold are sun on the waves: she is beautiful, there is no other word; no one like her. Myself, I am not handsome and I am older, ordinary. I have a potato face, but she has told me often that she loves it.

Visitors find us inexpressive, and this may be a result of the long years when to preserve one's self was to conceal it. But we two read each other well enough and I see a tremor pass over Liia's face as I talk about government—the faintest of frowns, just for a second as she bends forward over her plate. I have not yet told my wife that I see myself as a statesman eventually, an ambassador perhaps. Of course, it may not be possible. But I think I am as qualified as anyone else, and am beginning to build up the connections. Only last week I drank a beer with the Minister for Foreign Affairs.

I'll do it then? I say, meaning the dishes, which I also do on weekends. Toomis, why *ask*? she says. Then I am angry. She and I have run through gunfire across the Town Hall Square, and hidden in a cellar until morning. We have suffered countless indignities and wiped them away from each other in the night with words and caresses. We have not gone through all that, become free, in order to argue over greasy dishes. I want to tell her this and other things, I want to talk of the future, of international relations, of the possibilities, the right way to proceed. But she is not there. She has slipped away and back to her damned books. I almost want to take her by the shoulders (but they are so very thin) and shake her and say—

But I am not sure what, and I plug the sink with the bit of rag and fill it. We are making our own washing-up liquid now, faintly scented with something like lemons. The bottle is bright yellow plastic, with a picture of bubbles on it, though not so many come in reality. I search my mind for things I have read which might bear on the situation and I find nothing. Then I think that it is all over in five minutes and that if I can one day be an ambassador, to have gone to market and stood with my hands in greasy water on weekends will be neither here nor there. So long as I can take my place, I think, and this is a new feeling for me—I was before a medium and a repository for ideas, a memory, never a man of action. I realize that I am reading differently now: not all books interest me equally as they once did. I examine them for their use, their application. I see that I have already bypassed who I was, even though I seem to be the same and even though my circumstances are lagging behind me.

She works late in her room. I get out the bed and arrange the quilts and pillows for later. I go to the window. Karel from downstairs stands stock-still while his half-breed dog careens about in the night, its breath smoking.

On Monday, if the weather holds, the old women will be out with their twig brooms, clearing everything away, last year's rubbish, the weekend's dogshit. I see too that the old person in the torn coat is rummaging about in the bins again, pulling out the cardboard cartons and the bottles and putting them into separate carrier bags: another new thing. Lights burn behind the thin curtains. Most things are thin here and curtains are a good example: I have seen foreign ones in magazines, velvet drapes on heavy rails, but here they are scanty pieces of cloth or net which only gesture at concealment. I made our curtain hooks myself, bending them from wire. I am an intellectual and not a naturally practical man but circumstances compel. The flat opposite ours has a brand new white venetian blind, but that is very unusual and I wonder how they came by it. Carpets too are thin, not like the ones you find in hotels, and mostly clothes are thin as well, which surprises visitors. Coats are one exception: woollen, kapok-lined. Without such a coat, here you would die…Things, so many things.

I love my wife. I want her to come with me into our future. But the washing of dishes and the making of soup and the counting of books—surely, this trivia should not occupy so much of our time?

It is easier to talk in the dark. When finally she comes to bed I whisper my plans. She does not seem surprised—after all, she knows me well. You would enjoy the life, I say, would you not? You would make a fine ambassador's wife. We could live part of the year in a foreign city. We would be more at home in a cosmopolitan atmosphere, a city centre—an apartment with high ceilings, shutters, wooden floors, close to the cafés and shops. Perhaps a drier climate, milder winters. You could go on with your translations, of course, meet the writers and talk with them so as to get your text exactly right. Yes, she says, perhaps. You would like it, I tell her. The wallpaper would be on straight. The plumbing would be fixed. And neither of us would have to do the shopping and so on.

I love you, but you don't quite understand, she says.

What? What is it I don't understand? What?

We must learn to talk to each other differently now, she repeats.

Can some things not stay the same? It comes from outside, this, from something she is reading, but she will not tell me what. She says she is not ready to; it is difficult, she wants to be sure; she has always been careful that way.

I taught my wife English, in which she has since far surpassed me. I gave her personal tuition, because she was a gifted student and also because I liked to look at her. I remember explaining the tenses, the future conditional, the future in the past—all those tenses we do not have in our own language; they are hard to translate. I remember watching her mind work while her lips waited for the right word to come; I remember the dim light of the classroom, the creaks from the stove as it cooled and the metal contracted. In winter her lips were cracked, in summer they glistened. She was still a child. Afterwards I went home to my first wife, and lay next to her, and my young son was in the cot beside us. I lay sleepless the night through: I knew that there was more to life than I had expected, and there could be no peace until I had it.

And now at the beginning of spring neither of us sleeps. Our flat is near one of the few working lamps that stand like extra trees in the courtyard and pinkish light glazes the room. They have not yet installed individual switches and so the heating will be on until May; tonight it is far too warm, we have thrown the covers off and lie naked but not touching. The books we have read together, or separately and then told each other about, surround us. I am sometimes tired of books now, I whisper to my wife. I feel I have read enough for a lifetime. To say this feels like a confession.

Toomis, it is not the same for me. I am still looking, she says, lying on her back with her eyes open as if there were words on the ceiling for her to read—with her body open too, as if she read what was there with all of it, the soft skin of her belly, her tender nipples, the velvet between her thighs: all eye.

Tomorrow we will go to my mother in the country, eat lunch, help with anything she asks. We will bring home bags of home-grown potatoes, turnips and carrots, just as we did before Liberation and during it too. We do it always. But at the same time things are changing in ways I cannot predict. I was never afraid before, just angry and waiting. But I am afraid now, as I lie beside my beautiful wife. Silently I ask: Is this fear also the beginning of spring?

We, the Trees

S HE SHOULD HAVE SEEN TROUBLE coming from the way he stood out in the class. His hair, growing out of a short cut, was beginning to curl. He had the beginnings of a beard. He was one of many in jeans, dark T-shirt, and a green parka never removed however warm the room. But the way he carried himself was distinctive. She thought he might have trained as a dancer, or served in the military. Even sitting, he seemed taut, poised. During discussions, he constantly shifted position so as to see who was speaking and give that person his attention; he radiated a kind of alertness, physical and mental, that it was unusual to see in a classroom, especially at eight-thirty in the morning. But even so, there was nothing to suggest just how far he was preparing to go.

He asked for a consultation right after the first class.

"Well, sit down, Joshua," she said, removing some files from the spare office chair she had obtained from the

Humanities office upstairs. It was worn, but more inviting than the hard plastic item that was standard issue. "How may I help?"

"I chose this class because of your reputation," he said.

"For what?" she asked, amused.

"Open-mindedness," he told her, without missing a beat. "My final project is likely to be unconventional but I hope you'll be receptive to it."

"Do you want to say a bit more?" she asked.

"Not at this point," he told her. "I'm just giving you a heads-up. It's to do with the forest."

"The forest industry?"

"Not so much that," he said. "Well, there is one thing," he added, "we're not sure about paper."

"We?" she asked, but he just looked back at her, and she decided she had misheard. "An electronic file is fine," she told him.

"Actually, I feel I may want to speak it to you," he said.

"I'll still need the text," she told him, "to mark." He shrugged, and declined her proffered copy of the course outline for Journalism 200, which listed all the assignments, including the requirements for the final piece: a feature article of 2,500 words on a contemporary issue, showing evidence of a balanced approach, historical understanding, in-depth research, and judicious use of interview material: twenty marks.

At the door, Joshua paused, thanked her and smiled— and it was an extraordinary thing, that smile: it involved every part of his face, and could well have involved his entire body, too; it was blissful, intimate, infectious—to the point that she felt a shock of loss when the door closed behind him and her mood reverted to the norm, which suddenly felt closer to depression than she liked to admit.

It had been a *very* difficult year: her partner of fifteen years had moved out at the end of the previous semester, after months of emotional arguments over whether or not they should try to adopt. So now she was middle-aged, alone, and left to wonder, Was this it? What was she really for, now? Another twenty years of teaching? There were no prospects in the university, and it seemed to her that the industry she had once worked in had changed beyond recognition. Returning to it was a fantasy. But of all these voids and losses, the hardest to bear was that she was, now, extremely unlikely to become a parent. She made a point of taking regular exercise, and being as sociable as she could. Still, she often felt very low, and so that powerful, connective smile of Joshua's was very likely a good part of why she accommodated him when he followed an almost perfect first assignment consisting of an interview with a retired logger, *very personal but at the same time the history of an era and an attitude, sympathetic, humane, A+,* with a second piece that was completely off-topic, though in its way brilliant.

The assignment was for a *Who, what, where, when, why* piece covering a local event in 750 words. Instead, he handed in an essay called *Seeing the Woods for the Trees* which summarized a class discussion then argued that while the impossibility of objective "truth" in reporting was a given, the community could still come to an understanding that was what he called "closer to truth." He saw the journalist as inevitably partial, and morally bound to a frank acknowledgement of her bias or perspective, along with a rigorous attitude to fact-checking. Beyond that, the public must take responsibility to read widely and come to the best understanding possible through debate and conversation: the model of the writer as the one who created "truth" or "balance" was now obsolete. Each one of us, he wrote, had to find the way through the woods, to the trees, but we could not do it alone. Of course the argument was not new, but the writing, simultaneously academic and poetic—passionate, even, was striking.

The problem, she told him, was that he did not seem to have read the requirements for the assignment. There was no event. No particular *what, who*, et cetera.

"Not yet," he said. He kept his eyes on her face, but without seeming to stare.

"I wasn't looking for an essay," she told him. "You need to write about something specific. I gave examples. Look, I know you can do this, and I'll give you an extra week." At this, he treated her to another smile, a dose of warm human connection which briefly released the knot between her shoulders. However, no work materialized and after much struggle she gave him a C, which was both less and more than his piece deserved. Following this, he missed two classes, sending an email both times to apologize: he said he was in the forest, researching for the final project, which, for him, was the main part and only point of the course.

It was irritating to have her course ignored in this way, but she got over it, and warned him, as pleasantly as she could, that he was missing vital content and assignments which led up to that final project. In responce to this, he sent her a link to a published paper which sounded like a fantasy but turned out to be written by a well-respected academic at a sister university: the research showed how forest trees were joined to each other by a fungal web that connected their roots, and in this way were able to communicate their needs and share information and resources; every tree was interconnected by this mycorrhizal network and it was as if the forest had a vast, communal brain.

A TINY YOUNG WOMAN with thick brown hair in an urchin cut appeared at the next class. She introduced herself as Jen and said she had come to take notes and participate on Josh's behalf. She seemed to be familiar with some of the other students, and slotted right into the session on editing to a word count, though it turned out that she was not even registered with the university.

"You really can't come again," Paula told her. "But I'd be grateful if you could tell Josh he has missed another assignment now and his attendance is looking very poor."

"Josh is working very hard, I do know that," Jen said. "But I'll certainly pass the message on."

"Where is he?" Paula asked, but Jen was already halfway out the door, moving with a fluid, economical grace despite the heavy work boots that she wore.

That evening she received another email from Joshua: links to a set of maps showing the remaining areas of old growth forest in the world, compared to fifty and a hundred years ago. Shocking, she thought, but not news:

people had been protesting for half a century; global warming had been incontrovertibly attributed to human activity, yet nothing had changed. How many thousand stories had been written about this, while the weather became hotter and more erratic? Such writing was largely a matter of bearing witness, she understood that. But it was hard to avoid a sense of futility.

Thanks for your understanding, the note with the maps said, *I am counting on you.* Counting on you? For what? A passing grade? She felt it was something more than that, but as to what, she had no idea, and even though she was sitting in her overheated office with the light on, her skin tightened and she felt suddenly chilled.

I'm afraid I don't understand, she typed. *Your last three assignments are missing and although you are a very able student I am concerned about your progress in this course. Please let me know if you plan to complete the missing assignments. What I may do if I don't hear is refer you to Student Services, who ask us to identify students who may need support with the aim of meeting their needs...* She made sure to file a copy.

No reply.

Alex, very tall, with a slight stoop, greeted her at the door to her classroom. Just checking in, he said, offering his hand: it was calloused, and missing the top of the middle finger, but very warm. Josh was doing great, not to worry at all, he said. He was the most amazing guy, and what he was getting down was totally mind-blowing. So what exactly was he doing? Alex bent down to her level, lowered his voice. "Cross-species communication," he said. "I can't tell you more than that." He got out his phone and showed her a picture of Josh in outdoor gear posed with a pick and a shovel and other equipment in front of an enormous, gnarled tree-trunk so wide it filled the entire picture frame. His hair and beard had grown considerably, but even in the tiny underexposed image she felt as if he was looking straight through the screen into her eyes, his smile almost as captivating as it was in real life.

Cross-species communication? Josh had not seemed crazy or depressed, quite the reverse. She wanted to believe that he was engaged in some kind of eccentric but purposeful behaviour, that even now he might turn in a stunning piece of work at the end of the course. He had kept in touch, after all. But there was no reference to the missing work or to any desire to make it up, and another week had gone by. Clearly, she been too open-minded.

"Not attending," she told the counsellor at Student Services. "Three assignments missed, though he does communicate. He sends emails, maps, links to research papers about forest ecosystems, but no written work and no reference to it. No make-up plan. He's started to send his friends to class to take notes and bring me messages, like he's some kind of prophet in the wilderness. Well, it's getting to the point where I'd have to fail him even if the final project he keeps promising materializes and is brilliant…Struggling isn't the right word, he's very able, but even so, I thought I should let you know there's an issue here."

"It can't be overwork," the counsellor told her. "Joshua Pearson is only signed up for the one class, yours."

That's totally cool, he emailed her. *Thanks for your concern. I know this is hard to understand.* By this time, she had not seen him for almost six weeks and the course was entering its final phase.

What are your intentions? she asked. *Are you in some kind of trouble?*

Not at all, he replied, and then a girl called Angela dropped by her office to explain that Josh would not be in touch now until he finished. He had asked to be left alone for this final phase of his work.

"Why? What work, and where is he?" Paula asked.

"We can't say any more at this point," Angela told her. Her voice seemed to waver and her eyes were huge, the blue-grey irises floating in a sea of glistening white. "You'll be the first to know. Please be patient."

Patient? She made a second call to Student Services to update them. The counsellor said that they would do their utmost to contact him, and to rest assured, the matter was in their hands. Then she heard nothing at all for several weeks and although it was in a way a relief, she knew that she was waiting.

On the Friday when final assignments were due, she stayed late in her office to make a start on marking them. She had the blinds closed and a Bach violin concerto played softly in the background as she worked. Even through the music she heard her computer emit the soft chirp that signalled the arrival of an email, and without thinking, broke her rule about waiting until she had finished the current task before looking at the message.

This was the last email from Joshua (or rather, as she was later to realize, the last one sent from his account). It contained no explicit message, just the scan of a hand-drawn map showing logging roads and trails in a piece of privately owned forest land that lay three hundred miles north of where she sat. Directions to the forest were sketched in and then a route within it was marked with neatly drawn dotted lines and arrows pointing towards the destination, a red X. There were a few brief hand-written notes on the terrain, but no hint as to what the X marked. Leaning back in her chair, Paula let out a long sigh, closed her eyes.

I chose this class because of your reputation.

He had said that, in this very same room…And now, crazy or sane, he was relying on her to answer his call. *Because of your reputation.* She was being summoned. Why? What for? Should she go? Telling herself she would decide in the morning, she sent the document to print. But she knew that she had already made a commitment—or was it that he had made her make one? *Because of your reputation.* He had chosen her, and then, bit by bit, enmeshed her in something she did not yet understand. And now there was no choice: unwise as it might be, she would follow through and find the place marked X.

Early in the morning Paula packed her hiking gear and set off north, alone. It was a hard drive on twisting, hilly roads, much of it through managed forests in varying stages of growth. In some places, water ran down cliffs beside the road and covered it in a thin, shining layer. For miles on end, the road skirted a long, narrow lake. The farther she went, the slower she had to drive and the farther apart the occasional visible buildings were; exhausted, she put up on arrival in a motel mainly frequented by fishermen.

At first light she took a coffee and a pastry from the table in the lobby and drove to the trailhead. It was marked, just as the map indicated, with yellow tape. *Steep,* it said on the map, and it was hard going along a narrow path that rose steadily up the side of the valley. Light filtered only gradually through the canopy. Soon she was deep in the forest and enveloped by the peculiar, alert kind of silence found among trees on a still day. Now and then where there was a clearing and some lower growth, groups of small finches skittered from one tree to the next, and then in the wake of their passing the silence would gather itself back together. The light between the trees remained dim, uneven. The trail ran on thinly ahead, marked, as the map had promised, with little knots of fluorescent tape. The trees were second growth, but maturing, and densely planted: spruce, mainly, and red cedar. Beneath a thick layer of decomposing needles, the ground was tense with their roots. She came to a sharp downwards left turn, and had to scramble down a rocky channel that in worse weather would have been a creek. Now the trees grew bigger, mossier. The ground levelled out a little. A fall ahead created a slash of light, and she paused there to drink from her bottle and get her breath. She could hear running water nearby, which she took as confirmation that she had more or less arrived. This was the oldest part of the forest. There was a damp, fungal tang to the air now, an almost tangible odour. And next to her, a family of saplings grew out of a vast, rotting trunk. The mosses were extraordinarily green. This must, she thought, be the place in the photograph of Joshua that Alex had shown her, and she extracted her own camera from her pack and took a couple of shots of a vast tree to her right. She felt sure that Joshua had been here, and perhaps still was. But when she called out her voice was baffled by the trees and there was no reply, and no way other than on, deeper into the grove. Soon, the trail broke down and become many smaller, fainter paths winding through a stand of enormous trees.

"Josh?" she called again, standing still now. "Josh?"

And there, in the darkest part of the forest, she smelled his death. Her throat closed against a rush of bile, and a moment later she saw what remained of him: he was in a half-sitting position, his back propped awkwardly against the trunk of the vast, gnarled spruce. His legs were buried thigh-deep, as if he too had roots. She was sure it was him—though his face, with its awful bulging eyes, had swollen, and like the rest of him, darkened to the colour of a bruise. With the greatest effort she controlled the urge to vomit and noted that all around the body was a scatter of detritus—water bottles, a garbage bag, pillboxes, a blanket, some phials and syringes; his boots and socks, the shovel and pick used to dig the hole…Her heart thudded as she took a photograph, the flash bringing the scene into a sickly clarity. A box of some kind rested on Joshua's lap and it was, she knew, meant for her. Flies rose in a seething cloud as she drew closer: it was a plastic container, watertight, the kind made for camping. She should not open it: what would the police say? And yet how could she not? Forgetting the gloves in her pocket, Paula reached quickly for the box; his dead arm shifted as she took it and she half-ran, half-stumbled away from him, terrified—of death itself, of the silent trees with their huge trunks, their subtly connected roots.

She reached the mossy deadfall and stopped there, gasping, to empty her stomach. Afterwards, she pried the box open. Inside was a sachet of silica gel and a single sheet of paper, hand-written:

> We, the Trees
> Fair exchange. Leave us to stand.
> We care not about one or even several what matters is the sum of us and what matters is what passes between the sum of us and what passes between the sum of us and the sum of you. And in time all of you will become us and without us there is none of it.

The rain began, fat drops pattering on the leaves, and she was crying too. She looked up, wet-faced, at the patches of grey sky visible between the branches. Joshua was dead. A network of other people were involved. When it was released to the public, his message from the trees would, handled correctly, go viral in hours. This was Joshua's story: how he had sat there with his legs half-buried, trying to communicate, even to the point of self-sacrifice, and, as the end came, numbed himself with narcotics so that he could go on. This was his story, which he had thrust upon her and in which she, Paula Jacobs, had played a part.

Joshua Pearson had passed his work on to her. She must find Alex, Angela, and Jen and join with his network of friends and supporters; she must tease out the connections, unearth the rest of the story and then tell it, not just once but repeatedly: to the police, to the Dean, to Josh's heartbroken parents, to the court, to an endless series of interviewers on news and discussion programmes, at conferences, demonstrations—and then, when more and more young people went to the woods to die, she must continue to speak out in person, on screen, in print, online—she must and would use every possible medium to spread the story of their sacrifice.

Paula's hand shook as she reached in her pocket for her phone: there was, of course, no signal, and she left Josh there and began to run back through the trees.

Clients

I T'S A RITUAL: we shower, dress, turn off all devices, prise the lids from dips and spoon them into bowls, open rustling packets of vegetable sticks, hold wine glasses to the light. We enjoy the preparations and know Martin will arrive punctually at seven. We go together to the door and welcome him in.

A pale linen suit and faded terracotta shirt—undone as ever at the neck—set off the gleam of his rich brown skin. A tall man, he moves in a loose, underwater way.

Martin's first hour costs three times the subsequent hours, so we feel obliged to ourselves to take it in full. The higher rate, he's explained, enables him to be open-ended: to take just one booking per evening and then stay for as long as is required. Otherwise, he'd have to draw a line and depart for another appointment, which would loom over the whole evening, spoiling the feel of the occasion.

Folded elegantly onto the sofa opposite our two chairs, Martin tastes the wine, a very fine Sauvignon Blanc from New Zealand, and cocks his head. "Delicious!" he says. "Now, fill me in. What's new?" he asks, leaning forward in his chair, his eyes fixed on Anna's face as if she mattered to him more than anything in the world. And I find myself feeling that way, too. It's as if *I* had asked the question, and didn't already know the answer. It's as if her face comes into sharper focus as she prepares to speak.

"Work, well, so-so…" She tells him of difficulties with her team, how she had to repeat tasks, of a colleague who is trying to undermine her. Martin's face picks up each fleeting expression that appears on hers, and does to it something between amplifying and refining: something which lends it the same kind of dignity and grace which print can give to the written word. As one expression dies so another begins to grow, softly replacing it. His face is a perfect instrument and on it, we are expressed. What he says is quite ordinary. It's all in the way he listens.

"I know I shouldn't worry," she says, with a smile, a shrug.

"Don't you think anxiety is a substitute for action? The only things I worry about most are those I can do nothing about. Yet so much *is* within our control," he says. "And that is very liberating. It means we have more time—"

"But Martin," Anna interrupts, and his forehead puckers with her perplexity; he pauses mid-sip, "I never feel that I have *enough* time."

"Likewise!" I say, deadpan, the irony being that my job is, basically, to organize other people's time. Martin shoots me a brief, acknowledging smile and I feel myself relax.

"Well, look at it this way: centuries ago, all people did was work, eat, and go to church. That's history! Now I fret because I can't fit in scuba lessons on Fridays. So what is it you two don't have time for? Or shouldn't I ask?"

Martin's laugh is another wonderful thing, a benign infection, an invitation to bliss. You need do nothing but look and listen to join in, though tonight Anna does not. When he's finished she says:

"Sometimes I want just to waste time. Not know what I'm doing, what it's for."

"Taking Time to Do Nothing. I think I've heard of someone offering that as a workshop," Martin says. I join the conversation unbidden:

"But Martin, didn't people once just do *all* these things *themselves*?" And for a moment, just a moment, an anxious shadow, entirely his own, passes across his face. My heart pumps harder, as if I'd begun to exercise.

"Well, I'm sure they muddled along. But you do have to consider *quality*. I doubt that you two would enjoy a home-grown conversation, now, other than as a curiosity. Surely, it's better to reward someone for perfecting part of existence and making it into a service from which everyone can benefit?"

"Do you ever converse for free?" I ask.

"With friends, naturally," he says, back to his ordinary, calm self again. "But talk isn't something special for me. Work is work. You have pride in it, but it's a transaction:

you sell something to leave the rest of you free. Given my ancestors were slaves, I am relatively *very* happy with this."

"But now we're *all* slaves!" Anna half-rises from her chair.

"Hardly," Martin tells her. "And do you really want to go back to nature? Uninvent everything? Not so easy." Had he spoken oh-so slightly differently, those words might have been hostile, but he follows them with his warmest, most compassionate smile. My skin tightens; the hairs on my neck push against my shirt.

"But why not?" Anna's voice is rough with longing. And I too want time unorganized. However it comes. And I want her. I want her naked and wet, tangled, breathing hard. I want to abandon myself to her and then to pass into a shared sleep, a state during which no transactions of any kind occur. A void.

I want Martin gone.

"We all give freely to our children," he's saying now. "Are you two planning a family yet?"

"You pay for tests, for doctors," I tell him, "for creative play, for learning, for someone to mind them, for riding, ice skating, singing, counselling…Aren't they just new clients, in the end?" Martin's face, which is my face really, is so bitter that it frightens me.

"Stop!" Anna sits up straight, her chest forward, as if inhaling some new, enriched form of air. Just the thought of change makes her feel good. She turns to me, just me and says: "I'm sure it doesn't have to be like this. Let's try on our own, please."

I'd willingly drown in her green-gold eyes.

"I do know how you feel. I expect our capacity to do things for ourselves is atrophied, but anything is *possible*. What an interesting topic!" Martin glances at his watch. "Shall we continue?"

"No thanks, Martin," Anna tells him, and he smiles, then stands and straightens his clothes.

"You know," he says, "I've many clients who would take the whole evening on a regular basis. I'm beginning to find it scarcely worthwhile to do single hours.

"The apartment's looking good," he adds. "Who does it for you?" he says and then with a soft click, the door closes behind him, and we two stand for a moment, beached somewhere between shock and joy.

"Did you mean it?" I ask. She nods; we push two chairs close, sit facing each other, just so. Then she goes to dim one of the lamps. Then I get up, because I need to pee. We laugh at ourselves, finally settle in semi-darkness, the window slightly open, our backs cushioned, wine glasses on a small table we can both just reach. Silence bristles between us.

"Say the first thing that comes into your mind," she suggests.

"Toffee."

She giggles.

"You want some?"

"No. Toffee. Toffee," I repeat. A bubble of laughter forms in my throat. And I can almost feel the pull of *toffee* in my jaw. My mouth's wet, my tongue ready for whatever the next word demands. And she waits, watching my face, my lips, my throat. I have to swallow.

"Amber," she says. Language stretches between us, a new country, vast, intricate, ours. A glow spreads through us and, sculpting air with our tongues and lips, unravelling it with our ears and minds, in free exchange, we begin to explore all that seemed lost.

Lambing

WITHOUT LIKING HER MUCH, everyone agreed that it was a dog's life Ax Blaney led and meant by that that it was even harder than their own. The village was set high on the north side of a steep valley the colour of iron in winter and the colour of rust in the all-too-brief summer months. It was the kind of land that offered few possibilities, indeed only one: sheep. Generation after generation of the village's young had wondered, particularly on those days when wind ricocheted across the valley, strained against the semi-opaque glass of small windows set in the thick walls of houses built long ago by people shorter and tidier than themselves, why it was that those first settlers had chosen such a place to build. Yet it was a place which, when it came to it, few people had managed to leave. The single road, leading both to and from the village, was used almost entirely by those who came occasionally from the outside in, to deliver supplies, take away the mail or even, once or twice, simply by mistake. It couldn't be followed by the eye even halfway to the horizon: its colour melted into the mountain, it twisted and lost itself behind small hills, scree runs and patches of scrub. It was difficult to imagine going anywhere else.

LEAVING THE VILLAGE might have been Ax Blaney's best course of action when her husband Lark broke his thigh pulling ewes from a snowdrift and had himself to be dug out next day, frozen stiff in an attitude of pain and rage, but neither she nor anyone else thought of it. The West Moor and the yellow-eyed sheep that grazed it had been handed down from father to son in Lark's family longer than anyone could remember, and it came, not to Ax Blaney, but to Lark's brother Crow until such time as her sons were of age.

THOUGH THE VILLAGERS PITIED Ax Blaney, they also admired a hard man, and when Crow took it upon himself to interpret what might have been considered a mere stewardship as literal ownership for the next fourteen years, so leaving Ax Blaney with a stony half acre at the back of her house and two children to raise, no one thought any the worse of him. After all, she still had a roof over her head: hers was the very last cottage, standing a hundred yards or so from the point where the road finally petered out and became a track like any other. Provided she didn't remarry, she could live there the rest of her days and people would see to it that she and the boys didn't starve.

AT THAT UNCERTAIN MELTING point of the year between winter's worst and the beginning of spring, when the stored root crops were sour, the cabbages stiff with frost and, scooping out flour, her hands would hit the bottom of the bin, Ax Blaney would take daily walks halfway up the mountain and stand on a flat shelf of rock called the Slab. From there she could see many of the surrounding moors, each a separate territory painstakingly ringed with a stone wall and grazed by its owner's branded sheep. Even though the wind was fierce up on the Slab and the mountain still dappled with snow, she knelt, took her hands from her pockets, pressed them flat on the stone before her and wished. It was a private ritual but everyone guessed more or less why she went.

"Lark's wife is waiting for her runts," the women would say, keeping any traces of spite or contempt from their voices, for it could happen to any one of them. The men would more likely comment to each other, half-believing what they said, "Lark's wife's up there on the Slab—putting the Look on your ewes."

SINCE THE SPRING AFTER Lark's death, Ax Blaney had been offered those lambs in her neighbours' flocks which wouldn't suckle, were deformed, or for one reason or another seemed reluctant to grow. Tended carefully by herself and her boys, Ax Blaney found that many of these would survive and put on fat. Each spring she wished on the Slab and waited for the first bleatings to signal the start of lambing. The men were right in a way—she did indeed look at their gravid ewes and hope for the worst.

Blaney men had always been called after birds, and the twins could have expected to be Hawk and Eagle after their grandfather and his brother, but Ax Blaney had broken with tradition, naming her sons Right and Left because from their first days each had a distinct handedness, reaching for her unfailingly with one or the other miniature hand. In a village which admired men like Crow Blaney, the boys were regarded with some disquiet, for they kept to each other's company, were prone to weep and rarely fought. Crow should have stepped in to stiffen them but there again, people could see how it might be to his advantage if they grew up soft.

"A poor name brings poor growth. Too much mothering spoils a man," the women would say. "But what can she do? The woman leads a dog's life. Bringing nothing and past bearing: she won't wed again." Men did the picking in Roadsend, there were fewer of them. Turning their heads and spitting over their shoulders to avert bad luck, they summed up the situation more succinctly: "Runts."

Ax Blaney, however, seemed to like her boys how they were and took no steps to harden them as they grew into men. Softness seemed to characterize the Blaney household; it was their mark, the sign of their difference. Whilst other families wrested their living from the efforts of wiry, indomitable men on the harsh moors, fighting the wind, moving snowdrifts, standing waist-deep in streams, the Blaney's struggle was led by a woman and took place indoors around the fire, their feeble lambs cosseted inside for weeks, sometimes months, covered with blankets, petted and stroked, named, talked to, slept with and fed from bottles. There was not a year when the twins didn't weep together at the inevitable slaughtering, performed in the yard by their mother as they had no stomach for it and thought they would almost rather have starved.

AX HERSELF DISLIKED THE TASK—the lambs, grown into sheep but still clean and creamy, would follow her to their deaths, nuzzling at her legs and tripping over each other, skidding splay-legged on the flags in their natural eagerness and the last of their youthful high spirits. She stood with her legs astride them, and pulled their heads back to expose their throats, the whitest, softest part. At that moment, their yellow eyes would meet hers with an expression of such placidness that she herself sometimes could have wept from pity. They never struggled, but sank demurely to their knees in spreading lakes of blood, bright on the scrubbed stone. Yet she and the twins must eat, and the meat of those lambs cooked easily, was sweet and fat and tender as if the care that had been lavished on them repaid itself that way.

ON THE TWINS' FOURTEENTH birthday, which fell in November, Crow paid an unexpected visit. His wife Hammer had died only that spring. He brought with him a gift: two hats made from wool gathered from walls and bushes and spun by his younger daughter Sling in spare moments of the day. Ax served him with a bowl of soup. It was remarkable, people said, that though she had long had reason enough, and now more so considering that they were both raising their children alone—he with the benefit of two moors and two flocks and she on half an acre and a few runts—she never showed bitterness towards him.

Ax Blaney watched him in silence as he ate, his hands busy and his eyes down.

"That was good," he said when he had finished, and turned to Right and Left, who sat by the fire holding their new hats. They looked at each other briefly, as they always did before even the slightest of dealings with an outsider, then smiled warily.

"West Moor'll be yours this day next year," he stated, his eyes sliding from one pair of sky-grey eyes to the other.

"They don't know much," he said, turning back to face Ax. "Can't even work a dog. Send them to work with me and I'll put them in the way of things. Shearing, slaughtering—use of a knife."

It was common knowledge, and the source of much mirth, that Right and Left allowed their mother to slaughter. What was less well known was the quality and intimacy of life in the last house of the village: how the three of them sat around the fire late at night and could almost feel each other's thoughts with their eyes shut, how the thin soup they ate at the end of winter tasted to them better than anything in the world, how rarely they needed to argue, how often they laughed. Neither was it much appreciated that over the years all three of them had come to prefer their softness to the hardness outside, to be oblivious of pity, disapproval and their growing isolation. Ax Blaney had long since ceased to feel that she led a dog's life.

Even so, she weighed Crow's offer carefully for its advantages and disadvantages. What he said was true: although she let them help her, Right and Left were incapable of working the half-acre at the back of the house, let alone the moor, and she, though strong, was growing old. On the other hand, she was reluctant to send them to Crow, seeing as he'd already profited so much at her and their expense—and without even turning to look at their faces she knew that being taught by Crow to use a knife would seem to them a fate worse than death.

Crow felt in his pocket, brought out something wrapped in a scrap of chamois, and pushed it to her across the table.

"Open it," he said; then, when she hesitated, leaned across to do it for her. A small bone ring carved to give the impression of plaited rope lay on the soft leather. "This time next year we'll wed," he said.

Ax Blaney felt the weight of her sons' relief behind her as she pushed the ring back untouched. "Crow," she said, "me and the twins will stay as we are."

Crow pushed his chair noisily across the flags and walked to the door. "But you'll never do that!" he said. "The year those two are sixteen you can kneel on the Slab all you like but you'll find no one giving you runts. Why give, people will say, when they have the means to fend for themselves?" He left the door to bang in the wind.

Ax Blaney picked up the ring and threw it in the fire. "Don't you worry," she said as they watched it, a black band in a burst of flame, burning hard and long, "we'll stay as we are."

THAT NIGHT THE FIRST SNOW came and Ax, sleeping in a chair by the fire was wakened as always by the sudden silence it brought. Right and Left slept on a mattress of lambskins; she had made it years ago, and since then they had grown beyond all expectation so that their legs stuck out almost to the knee. They lay on their sides, facing each other so that each would see the other on first waking. She rose and pulled the blanket over them, feeling its thin-ness, the weight of her promise—its impossibility, the twin impossibility of betraying it.

Crow was pleased with his evening's work. "She'll turn," he commented drily to Sling and his son Gull. "She'll have to. Come the spring after next she'll be banging on our door." He made sure as well to inform the rest of the village of his offer, long expected, and its refusal, utterly unforeseen.

"Who does she think she is? If she won't be shorn, she'll have to be skinned," commented men and women alike. It was easy to avoid the last house in the village. "She may feed runts and put them in a feather bed, but we've no need to. She can put grass in her soup."

That spring, Ax received only half the usual num-ber of ailing lambs, and those were left anonymously by night at her door. The superstitious sympathy which had tempered the villagers' contempt for difference vanished, and tongues long bitten back ran free. "A woman that slits sheep brings a long winter and a year of foot rot," said the men, leaning on walls of stone crusted with pale lichens, built by their fathers' fathers, "but she'll turn."

Indeed, the next winter was particularly harsh. Day in, day out a thin column of smoke rose from each stone chimney. The road was blocked from late October, and although the sky was often almost unnaturally bright, shining like blue ice over the iron-coloured foothills, with their long shadows and the drifts of white in the valleys, those early snows endured for many months.

The flocks gathered in sheltered corners, cream against white and grey, their marks—crimson, viridian, Prussian blue—like wounds on the side of a huge beast, sleeping or dead. Many were slaughtered out of season.

Late in February, the weather suddenly broke. Free of care, Crow and the villagers eagerly awaited lambing, Ax Blaney's appearance on the Slab, and the submission to follow. Ax, however, stayed at home, swept her yard carefully, took out the last piece of salt meat and put it to stew with some barley.

"This is the last of it," said Right, throwing mean scraps of peat on the fire. They both looked up at her, questioning.

"Don't worry. Put it all on. Eat," said Ax, setting the bowls before them, taking none herself. She watched them carefully. How fine their faces were, so little touched by wind or rain or rage, and caught now in the first yellow sunlight of the year. How soft their hair.

"Is this the last?" asked Left, hesitating before refilling his bowl. "Will there be lambs this year?" How perfect the set of their shoulders, the clear gaze of their grey eyes, which met hers suddenly, calm, trusting and content; how much she loved them, how angry she was that every last thing should be taken away.

"There will," replied Ax, her eyes shining. "Eat."

After, she told them to leave the dishes, and asked them to come out into the yard. A single star pricked the darkening sky above their house.

"Look!" she said, pointing upwards with her left hand, and with her right, firm from practice, she slit their throats.

IT WAS CROW WHO DISCOVERED why Ax Blaney, seen several days in a row preparing the ground of her half acre for vegetables, had stopped growing thin and hadn't come to knock on his door. Impatient and troubled, he went to knock on hers. Ax invited him in, just as before. A fierce fire roared extravagantly in the grate, and arranged symmetrically on each side of the chimney—the largest pieces at the top, the smallest at the bottom—joints of meat hung smoking; enough to feed a family all year.

"Do they taste sweet to you, my sons?" said Ax softly. Blanching, Crow dropped his spoon on the table; the feeling of nausea kept him in his chair just long enough to reappraise the situation.

"The Moor'll be mine in any case," he said slowly, "but I've still need of a wife. Sling's but thirteen and she's expecting. I'll need a grown woman's help and more room when the time comes." He picked up his spoon and deliberately took another mouthful of soup. "So. We can say the twins were lost on the peak. They'd never have learned in any case." Ax reached across the table and tipped the soup in his lap.

"Get out," she spat, realizing for the first time that it would have been worth struggling to slit Crow's unsightly throat instead of those of her twins, so easy, as they gazed upwards at the sky. And only days later, when she watched the column of cavalry and the magistrate in his carriage, hidden then reappearing, seeming one minute nearer, the next farther, but nevertheless always coming closer, did she realize that the road which brought them to her could have taken both her and her sons away.

Woodsmoke

THE THIN MAN HAD COME into the café, late, four days in a row. Each time he drank only a small coffee and a glass of water. But that day he ordered a lemon cake as well and ate it quickly without using the fork, leaning over the table and pressing his finger onto the plate to pick up crumbs. His skin seemed sallow against the white of his shirt, a foreigner, I thought, though I couldn't tell what kind, and not a tourist. From the way he spoke, in a careful, educated way, I knew that it must be a long time since he came from wherever it was he belonged to: a dry country, I guessed, mountainous, where people lived scattered thinly among their sheep and goats, were careful and burned fires all year long. Where the single city was full of the sound of bells; the streets lined with country people selling fruit and bolts of cloth. An old, quiet place, with cars only for the important people—not sunny, not bright with chrome and neon like here. I was very young then and I liked only new things.

The first time he had appeared I was angry. Summer was over; people went home early: often not a single customer pushed through the glass doors after eight o'clock, so that I could eat, sweep, and still have thirty minutes to sit on a stool with my shoes off and my books open. But as it turned out, the foreigner was never a nuisance: he did not put on the jukebox and he did not expect to talk to me the way most men did. He simply sat with his back to the mirrored wall and looked out of the window towards the sea, or read a newspaper. When I turned off the lights behind the bar, he would shift slightly in his chair. When I went to pick up the chairs and stack them upside down on the tables, he took his own cup to the counter, before wishing me goodnight and leaving me with five minutes still to sweep the floor. So I had grown used to him and that evening, when I looked up from my book and saw him sitting there still as one of the stones on the beach, I asked:

"Have you been here long?" His answer: "eight years" overlapped the question as if he had been waiting for me to speak. He rose quickly to his feet and brought his cup, plate and glass to the counter, although there were still fifteen minutes to nine.

"I am working at the hospital," he continued, "just started. Paediatrics. It took me six years to re-qualify, although I was fully trained in my own country and head of a department, in fact."

"I am studying too," I told him as I put my books away. "Languages. But I can't do it full-time. It will probably take me sixty years to get my degree, so don't complain."

"You're from the country," he said.

"Maybe," I told him, because I didn't like it that it showed still; I had felt, ever since I came to the city that I didn't belong back there, with the perpetual dust and the lame cattle and the bent old women, the men with no teeth, but in the places they taught us of in class. The foreign man smiled in a quick, shy way that I liked: so different from the slow grins of the local men. I surprised myself by saying:

"Would you like to come home with me?"

"Yes, please, I would," the man said.

WE WALKED QUICKLY through the streets and up the stairs to where my two rooms were: the small kitchen with its Calor stove and stone sink, the other with my books, table and folding bed. The shower was on the floor below. I poured some wine. We sat side by side on the cream lace spread that Grandmother had given me before I left. I unbuttoned his shirt. His skin was a pale, woody brown, not honey-coloured like mine nor rich chocolate like that of the man before him. I pressed my face into its warmth, breathed him in. He smelled like something burning, like woodsmoke, part bitter, part mystery. And his nipples, when I found them with my lips, were also bitter. But it was a kind of bitterness that was almost sweet in the way that it made me want to taste more of it: I leaned into him, slipped one hand around to his back, running my fingers down the side of his spine. I pushed against him, wanting him to lie down so that I could sit astride him and look down into his face. I was sure in my bones that this foreigner would be a good lover, sensual, considerate. But he resisted me and sat there quite straight on my bed.

"I had to leave my own country," he began suddenly. I could feel his voice vibrating in his chest. I wanted him to touch me now, not to talk. "I went in a hurry, because of the regime," he continued, and I knew that I ought to ask him where it was, and what regime, and what they had against him; I knew that at the very least I ought to want to know what language it was that he spoke there. But it was a long time since I had brought a man back to my room. I eased his shirt away from his shoulders, breathing in the smoky smell of him.

"I had a wife," he said, "who died." Then, I had to stop. I straightened myself and looked into his face. He looked down.

"I am sorry," I said and I told myself that this wife was in the past tense and had he not, after all, come home with me? "You do want to make love?" I asked, and there was a long pause. He looked over my shoulders into the corners of the room.

"After all, I don't think so," he said. My body felt cheated, yet he relaxed and smiled, as if something good had happened. He reached behind him for his jacket and took out a photograph. "That's her," he said "those—are the children." I looked: a slender woman and the two children, one girl, one boy about three and four, were wearing ordinary western clothes and sat, smiling, in front of an intricate geometric pattern painted onto a plastered wall.

"I'm sorry," I said again. But I did not ask him their names, nor where the children were, although I felt that this was what he wanted. He put the photograph back into a leather wallet tooled with patterns like those on the wall in the photograph and in silence we finished the wine. Then he put on his crisp white shirt and buttoned it up. I watched while he rinsed the glasses out under the tap.

"I'm sorry I haven't been more help," I said at the bottom of the stairs.

"Really, it's nothing," he said and suddenly he hugged me very tight so that I could smell the smokiness of him again, even through his clothes. Then he was off, walking rapidly down the narrow street which smelled of other people's evening meals. I went back upstairs to my books.

Much later that night, as I lay on the narrow bed looking at the street lamp opposite, it came to me that for certain I was the middle one of three. The stranger would have made love with the woman before me, sensually and with consideration, several times, and in the morning, over their hurried coffee on the way to work, he would have told her about leaving his country, but not about his wife and children. When he never returned, that first woman would have felt angry and far more cheated than I myself had, just a few hours ago.

The one after me, he might meet in one month's time or in ten years' time. They would not go home to his place or to hers, but sit in a calm room or a bench in the flower gardens in the city park, or even opposite each other at a quiet time in an ordinary, smartish café like the Oasis. He would tell her that he had left his country in a hurry, because of the regime. He had to pay four months' salary for papers. How he had crossed the mountains on foot in winter; two of the others had died. He had spent six months in a transit camp. He would explain how he had received one letter from his wife, bravely telling him not to worry and that it was for the best, she understood. But he did worry, of course, as the months passed with nothing more from her and each new arrival telling how much worse things were at home. Then someone came who had witnessed it: a sharp winter's day with dogs barking and the quiet street suddenly full of soldiers and noise. She told him the number of his house and the colour of his wife's hair. And what about the children? You asked, and so I must tell you, the witness said. Them too.

You could never know for sure what would have happened if he had stayed. He might have survived: if he had, in hiding perhaps, for how long would he have been able to save his family? Might not his presence have made things worse for them? Perhaps his wife would have suffered more if she had known he was in prison? Maybe he, a married man, should never have challenged the regime? Shouldn't he have thought of the consequences, bided his time?

It was impossible to judge. But also it was impossible to deny that he had left them behind; that they had met their deaths without him. With this third woman the stranger would weep, and she would too; perhaps they would make love, perhaps just once, but in any case they would be friends for the rest of their lives.

I remember lying there on my bed, with my hands behind my head, somehow knowing all this and thinking at the same time with another part of my brain how I would graduate, competent in Spanish, German and Russian, fluent in English, which is still what everyone wants. Then I would stop working at places like the Oasis Café and see the modern world with my own eyes. I aimed to eventually specialize in simultaneous translation for conferences and so on, so even after I had finished my degree there would be more to learn. I had already looked into it: one year in London, if they accepted me. Oh, I badly wanted to ride in aeroplanes and stay in hotels on expenses.

All of that has come true. I am sitting in a hotel bedroom now, with a fridge of drinks and twenty channels to choose from. It's the last evening and there have been no complaints about the interpretation, which amounts to praise. I sit here in my dressing gown, smelling of Chanel, and consider myself.

I have always sent money to my younger sister, who looked after Grandmother until she died (also, I send glossy postcards of each new country I visit) but in thirteen years I have never returned to see them in the village. I even missed the funeral. I was afraid that if I returned I would never escape again.

Laughter comes from the bar below and they are not so bad, these engineers, not really. I could go down if I chose, but I do not. Instead I sit here and think of the place I find myself calling home, and of my incredible luck: even if all of us smell of smoke, I think, only some can go back, and I am one of those. And the red dust path, winding like a lazy S, is still there, and the well, and the branch house under the tree, and in it my sister—though older, and still angry with me—splitting sticks for the fire. I sit here and think of the smell of the stranger. Of what he told me. How different I would be with him now.

I Like to Look

I HADN'T SEEN OR HEARD of her for fifteen years. No one had. We sat in the garden, spaced equally around the circular table: she to my right and Bill, the man who brought her, to the left; in the middle a jug of lemonade. Their big red car gleamed in the drive. I wouldn't let them inside the house.

"I've been all around the world, some of it in a very small boat and some of it I even swam," said my sister Dee, folding her sunglasses away and examining the garden: walled, thick with shrubs and so much smaller than the world. "Listen. I've been in an army. I've lived with pygmies and Eskimos. I've—"

She was thinner than I remembered her, her skin darker and drier. Her ears had been pierced and she wore studs that looked like pearls and real gold, but it was her all right: her eyebrows still scattered across the bridge of her nose, her nails were still bitten close. I could see the right thumb, pointed from too much sucking as a child, the scar on her forefinger from the time she'd thrust it experimentally into a light socket. Me, Mother, Dee, and our brother: once we all lived here. Now Dee and I sat side by side in the garden of the yellow-stone house which she left, in which I still live. The windowpanes are wartime glass, faulted so that the whole world can seem drunken-strange; on stormy days seaspray lands on them, dulling my sight, like cataracts.

"I performed an appendectomy with a penknife," she continued. "I can speak eight languages. I've made love to nine people simultaneously—the men were all tied up and gagged. But best to begin at the beginning: I started off picking avocados, then I was on one of those trawlers that freeze the fish then and there. Herring. Once we were caught in the ice—"

"You always said that travel was what you'd like to do," I interrupted. "You always did like getting about."

"You…" She faltered, as if she couldn't quite remember me. "You didn't. You were odd. You used to sit and just stare into space."

"You've not been there then?" I asked.

"Listen," said Dee, drawing herself up straight, "I just thought I'd look you up. The rest of them can go to hell, but you, I thought you'd be interested." The man called Bill leaned over suddenly and kissed my sister on the lips. The pores around his nose were large and open. He had purple flecks on his cheeks and even on the lids of his eyes. His hair had been artificially streaked. Their lips squirmed wetly. My sister closed her eyes. A cobweb of saliva stretched between them, then suddenly broke as they pulled apart.

"What are you looking at?" Bill asked me angrily, wiping his mouth on his sleeve. I thought it was obvious. I saw that one of his teeth was chipped, and a line was beginning to cross the bridge of his nose, the flesh plumping up to either side of it.

"You're still doing it!" he said.

"I like to look," I replied. And then I thought: yes, that's what I do. Looking. I like to look. So I kept on looking at Bill, and saw how the ridge of his jaw was patchily shaved, the stiff hairs, just grey, growing through in clumps.

"For God's sake!" he said, turning his face away.

"Don't mind my sister," said Dee. "Listen. Bill's a director and he's going to make a movie about me, the story of my life and my adventures. Aren't you? I dived for these pearls myself. There's so much to tell.

"I spent twenty-nine days alone in the Gobi Desert. I've got a pilot's licence. I tickled the soles of the feet of the Dalai Lama for nearly an hour and, believe me, he didn't move a muscle. I've been in three movies, but you won't have seen them: it was in Turkey. I lost half a million dollars at cards. Wasn't mine, but it would have been if I hadn't lost it. Easy come, easy go. Look at my arm, see? It was done in Hong Kong by a bearded lady. Took over forty hours. And look at the muscle too. I took cyanide in a hijack death-pact and came to just as they were about to bury me. I've got three passports. I didn't do much in the antipodes—too burnt out. Lived in a cave, had a baby, got it adopted, joined a theatre group. Then I met the sheikh—"

Bill refilled our glasses. The ice had melted into small slivers; it was old and made the drink taste faintly of metal. Dee paused to swallow.

"What about you, er—" Bill said, "do you share your sister's passion for adventure?"

"Yes," I replied, "but—"

"She was always the quiet one," Dee cut in. "It was the sheikh, you see, who gave me the half a million. He wanted to marry me, but I slipped out one morning and left for Canada. Now this might have got back: I killed someone in a bar in Montreal. Self-defence. I was tried, but I got off, of course. You didn't hear? After that, I went to the Soviet Union, as it was then, in the summer, mind you. I left, my jacket padded with manuscripts, just before they kicked me out."

Yes, I thought, I like to look. In trains, buses, gardens, at films, even those in languages I don't understand, on pavements and curbstones, in mirrors and water there's much to see and I look. I look at faces, the folds around eyes, the sculpture of flesh that grows with time to reflect habits of thought and feeling, the many textures and colours of skin. I look at litter, wet paper, September leaves. I look at the sea: sometimes the sky is darker than the water, a negative. Sometimes the beach is smooth and damp, and as the sun sets the sand blazes brazen-gold. On the rocks, mussels build themselves into tight black bouquets. I like to look at the fossils, exposed in shale that softens, blurring in a matter of hours the sharp record of past millennia, dissolving them within a day. I like to look at the shadows of twigs mingled with clots of leaves, just stirring in the wind. At sand blown around grasses and debris, at frost on windows, at gulls landing like a scattering of crumbs on the sea. I like to look at the wind seen through glass, at the flow of traffic, its motorway lights tailing into the distance, red retreat, oncoming white.

"Miles away," Dee said to Bill, meaning me. "We're twins, you know."

"You're not at all alike!" Bill said to Dee, conspiratorially.

No, we're not. She left, I stayed put. She has a story to tell; I sit and stare, look and see. While she was away I saw some sights. I saw our mother shrink. Her skin grew yellow, a damp envelope. I saw the snowdrops each spring. I saw a last breath, and the skin growing luminously pale. I pulled back the sheet and looked upon our mother's bones, seemingly wrapped in bleached and shrunken cloth. I saw our brother, taller than any of us and fitter too, trying to catch sparrows in his useless hands. I looked at rainbows in soapsuds stretching and bursting, at a tangle of earthworms, wet, glistening; saw the scars where their ends had grown back. I saw the yellow stone of our house obscured by ivy, how the small dry roots pushed themselves into its pores and cracks. I looked at myself in the mirror and felt that it would break; I looked longer and the feeling went away.

Dee leaned closer towards me over the table.

"I spent three months in the Pacific Basin, stuck because of storms. I got married to an island chieftain, not that it counts now I'm back. Free as a bird—" She threw her head back and laughed. Dee, I thought, if I had been around the world, I would have seen a great deal more than you. That's but one of my bitternesses.

"I've dined with kings," she continued, "with shamans, beggars, gods incarnate, lunatics and transvestites. I've had more diseases than I can remember, unnamed fevers, various malarias, malnutrition, amoebic dysentery; in Nepal my liver grew so huge that it threatened to squash my lungs. My skin turned orange. I thought I would lose a leg…"

Looking. It isn't only a passive pleasure, a drinking in. Looking can be hard. Looking can vanquish time. Looking can change water to wine. It can wipe fear clean away: I have looked at entrails on the road until my gorge no longer rose and choked me, and now I can distinguish them and their circumstances. Looking can turn another's eyes away. Looking can strip skins, drain blood. Looking can abolish the other. There's a power in looking. I've discovered it over the years, and that day in the garden was the first day when I realized what I had, and the only time I dared its use.

Dee's glass was empty. She sighed, and smiled at us both. White flecks had collected at the corners of her mouth. Bill was sweating, the top of his collar grey and damp.

"Why did you come back here?" I said.

"To see you, of course," she lied, "and the house."

"Yes," said Bill, pushing back his chair, "I'd like to see the house."

"You can't film this house. It's mine until our brother dies." I spoke without turning to look at him. "Perhaps you'd like to see him? Seeing as the garden is so secluded, I let him go naked in the summer. He can't speak. His face is slack, his body going the same way. His appetite is enormous."

"Will you stop staring at me," snapped Dee, glancing down at the bracelet of pearls which she had dived for herself through a world of impossible colour, blue and yellow fish, purple corals shimmering with refracted light. She was growing very pale. I looked, I looked hard for a very long time.

"I used to think you were beautiful," I said softly. She was about to continue her account of places been, not seen. And then she would have made her request again, more forcefully. Her eyes were glancing offside, to check that Bill was listening; her grainy tongue-tip poked through parted lips, moist with bitter lemonade. I looked.

"Dee?" Bill leaned forward, touched her arm, grasped her wrist. His fingers left no mark. Then he ran from the garden, and the red car sped off down the coast road, clashing with the sea and sky.

Those lips are dry now, Dee. Leaves whirl around your legs. Dirt collects in the crook of your arm. Rain runs clean tracks over your face. Salt spray ages you, scouring at the sharpness of your features. Sometimes our brother pisses on you when I've locked him out; at other times he picks flowers and lays them at your feet. He at least, I think, can do what he wants. Dee, I am all eyes, and you are still and home at last, forever in the garden: not flesh, nor bone, but stone.

Saving Grace

THE ROAD SLICED ACROSS the map, narrow but determined. There were no junctions, no land-marks, no settlements of any kind until it reached the small eminence upon which was built (supposedly, thought Libby—it seemed the right word for the day) the regional capital, Wantwick. That was their destination. They would know when they got there, or so she hoped. She drove, the other two ominously quiet. Sally had said she would take a turn at the driving, but she kept her eyes shut and seemed to have forgotten about it. On either side of them were large fields planted with some kind of grain which seemed to grow very unevenly, leaving bald patches of stony-looking soil. Above them the huge sky had been scoured clean of cloud by the wind.

"Can't we stop?" said Clark suddenly. "Look. On the left. It says 'Tea.'" Libby swung the van down the track. Stray ears of corn and clumps of poppies were growing through chalky rubble. There was no evidence that anyone had been there for a very long time.

"Wild goose chase," said Clark, "the whole thing, I mean. Not just the tea." Libby glanced at him in the mirror. The corners of his mouth were drooping. He rarely left the city. Another two hours and he would be demanding they went home. He knew he was indispensable. "Nothing could happen in a place like this," he muttered, "nothing. Scarcity of people is one reason, hideousness is another. And no cell phone service! You know they're asking for independence? Imagine!"

Libby hoped they arrived soon. Somehow, the farther they got from base, the less her seniority seemed to count.

"Even when the Revenue give the place a wide berth. Should've cleared it right up and used it for dumping," said Sally, adding brightly, 'It's just the sort of place where you'd go mad, isn't it?"

The track narrowed, grew suddenly muddy, turned sharply to the left, then came to an end between two gates. A rusty estate car was parked facing them. A notice taped to the windscreen said "Tea here," and behind it a woman sat in the driver's seat, reading, one elbow protruding from the open window. There was a pile of newspapers on the passenger seat. The one the woman was reading, Libby noticed, was parchment-yellow and dated last January.

"I'll need to get past you," the woman said. In the back of the car she lit a small stove, decanted water carefully from a plastic container and unwrapped some mugs packed with newspaper in a cardboard box. Her face was pretty in a tense, pointed kind of way: almost a city face. Beneath the bulky jacket, Libby guessed, her body would be small, but powerful. She felt a brief stab of guilt that this woman should be immured in her rusty car, day in day out marooned in such an empty tract of land, reading old newspapers, whilst she had her own office, use of an up-to-the-minute van, the services of Clark—despite his sulks, the best cameraman available—and, most important of all, control of a budget. And she'd only had to come here—Clark was right, godforsaken was the only word for it—because something had, for once, happened. Supposedly. There could be nothing worse than selling things to earn your living, she thought, and the more mundane the product, the more tiresome it must be. Buying was far better.

"Do you do much business?" she asked.

"Where're you from?" the woman replied, glaring at the stove.

"We're from NTV," Libby said—this normally warmed people up—"come to do a feature about a woman in Wantwick. We are on the right road, aren't we?"

"You'll have trouble," the woman said, pouring water, steaming but far from the boil, into a metal teapot. "Three of you? That'll be nine ninety."

"That's rather a lot," said Libby, but she was already reaching for her pocket.

"You get a biscuit with it."

"How far is it to Wantwick?" asked Libby, humbly.

"'I can sell you a map if you want," the woman replied, handing her the mugs. "Don't forget to bring them back."

"I'm not drinking this!" Clark said. Sally bit experimentally into her biscuit, then spat the residue out of the window. It would hardly be possible, Libby thought, to forget about returning the mugs with the woman staring at them like that, as if they were criminals. Neither was it possible to persuade one of the others to take them back: "Too cold," Sally said, nestling up to Clark.

"I might want to buy the map, but could I see it first?" Libby asked as the woman upended Sally's mug and began to dry it out with newspaper. She gave no sign of having heard. Defeated, Libby returned to the van.

She drove on. Sudden gusts of wind sent the corn flat and could be felt even inside the van, pushing against the steering and sneaking in through the vents. The landscape was as unyielding as a line drawn firm across paper with a ruler and square. Couldn't be much fun—even for the few people that did live there. Supposedly. And no tourist trade, as in the other empty lands to the north and west. Even before the Commission it had never been densely populated, but there must have been towns, villages, and single, unproductive dwellings growing steadily more unreachable as the roads fell into neglect: all flattened now under the hot gale of economic and demographic rationalization that had swept the country—flattened, and then sunk more thoroughly than the ghost towns of other waves of progress, now under reservoirs with their tolling bells and telltale morning mists, or wrapped in lava and preserved for everyone to see.

A turbulent time that must have been: Libby could remember some of the slogans and feeble protests—or were those perhaps her parents' memories, absorbed in the blood? It has been as hard and fierce as the one outside, that wind of change, but now everything was settled, like dust falling softly where it had to rest. People lived where they were needed and all the land was used according to demand. There was no waste. It was a country that led the world.

We could be anywhere, thought Libby. If I couldn't feel the engine running and see the figures creeping up on the clock, I'd almost think we were standing still. And there were those signs of course, not direction signs, but every ten miles or so a small track joined the road, each bearing its handwritten advertisement: "Beans 700 yards," "Good Rubble," "Oven-Ready Tame Rabbits," "Cut Flowers," "Manure," and so on. Presumably a rusty car and a surly woman waited at the end of each, like a spider in its web. Behind her, the crew were quiet. Neither of them had wanted to come, and indeed, thought Libby, the journey seemed much longer than she had expected.

"I think we're nearly there," she announced at last. It was dusk. The other two were both asleep. Spitefully, she opened the window and let in the sharp air. For the first time, a vehicle passed them going the other way, and ahead was a misty cluster of lights on the horizon. "There must be a hotel," she said.

"Fortunately," said Clark, "I have a chocolate bar which I am prepared to divide more or less equally among the three of us."

"For God's sake, stop it," snapped Libby. They passed a sign which said, in short fat letters without any welcoming messages or traces of civic pride, *Wantwick*.

"He's got a point, Lib," said Sally. "It's not a place famed for its hospitality. Or anything, come to that."

"We're here to work, not enjoy hospitality," said Libby. Her neck ached.

"It better be something special, though, hadn't it?" Sally said sweetly. "This woman better be getting up to something stunningly good, because we can't exactly rely on the glamour of the location. What gave you the idea?"

"George!" snapped Libby.

"Him Himself? You're sure it wasn't one of his little jokes? Look—over there." Clark's voice was weary. "The orange 'H' followed by half a 'T' might be what we want."

THEY SAT IN THE ROOM and shared Clark's chocolate and some whisky he had brought as well. Three single beds were ranged against one wall. Periodically the table light went out and had to be fed with coins. There was no television.

"For this money we'd stay in the best place in town, *à la carte*, movies, piano and dancing thrown in."

"It's freezing." Sally climbed under the covers of the bed nearest the door.

Libby kept silent. It wasn't the time to mention the odd juddering that had beset the van after she turned the engine off, nor her suspicions that it would not start in the morning, nor her worry that Sally might well have put her finger on it about George sending her here out of spite. He probably knew she was after his job.

"The bookcase is locked," reported Clark. "*For reading, apply at reception.*"

THEY ARRIVED AT THE WOMAN'S house on foot. It was in an old municipal estate, a rarity in the rest of the country but apparently still used here—where fresh investment was scant, and people not as fussy. Libby had to carry the camera. Clark and Sally had slept together, or tried to, and kept Libby awake as well. She didn't think they'd enjoyed it much, but it had probably kept them warm. They hadn't had any breakfast, because none of them could stand the hotel one minute longer.

The house was falling to bits, but the sign outside was better done than most in the street. *The Truth. Here. Cheap, Plus Free Gift!* Clark laughed sardonically. It did look pretty lame.

"Just turn that thing on," said Libby, "and take some shots. We can jazz it up later." If I've been sent on a fool's errand, she thought, I'll bloody well turn the tables. Dragging the other two with her, she strode past a queue of about a dozen people, all sandy-haired, short and wrapped in long, oatmeal-coloured coats, who were waiting by the gate, and up to the front door which was ajar. As she reached it, a stone bounced off the frame.

The woman, quite old and shrunken, was wearing a faded plaid dressing gown and sitting on a straight-backed chair in one of the upstairs rooms. The room was otherwise empty but for a corner cupboard and a couple of large empty boxes, animal cages of some kind, with wire mesh stapled across their fronts. She stared at the three of them—obviously city people in their bright coats and scarves. Clark and Sally were sharing one of Clark's jokes—"The Truth is strangely apparell'd"—shaking with laughter as they set out the camera and lights.

"Those two won't get out of Wantwick alive," the woman said, suddenly but without malice, gesturing at Sally and Clark.

"That's *true*," a voice sang gaily. It was coming, very obviously, Libby thought, from the cupboard in the corner. You could see a bit of dressing gown, like the old woman's, sticking out under the door.

"Good morning," Libby said brightly, although her heart was sinking, "we are from NTV." Sally set the lights on, flooding every corner of the bare room. The woman didn't so much as blink. The camera was up and running.

"You're a fool-girl," the woman said, matter of fact, without venom, "stumbling in, jumping queues and breaking the rules. Bringing a pair like that with you."

"Very true," the voice sang again.

"I do apologize. Your fame has travelled, so to speak. Can we please watch you work?" asked Libby, smiling as hard as she could. "We'll pay," she added.

"I know that. Stay as long as you like. That won't be long. None of your plans will come to fruit, you'll fail completely." The woman's baleful stare seemed to enfold them all like a thick, stifling blanket. "You think you're lucky to live in the cities. You think it's kinder there and people are more generous, but that's only because they've got more. You're stupid, and you're deeply mean. You don't like your friends drinking too much of your wine. You count up favours and drop people if they don't pay you back. You're jealous of your sister Phil." At this, Libby blushed and tried to interrupt. "You're proud of yourself and fuck knows why. Your work's junk. You'll believe any old rubbish so long as it profits you. You'd sell yourself to get the Station Controller's job. You're snobbish, pig ignorant and eventually you'll get cancer. But you do look nice, nicer than us in Wantwick, all three of you do."

"That's all true." They didn't sound so stupid now, whoever it was hiding in the cupboard.

"What about the free gift?" Clark's voice was fainter than usual.

"You haven't paid yet," said the woman without looking at him.

"How much?" Libby was already reaching into her pocket.

"Everything you've got," the old woman, said, "and then you can get out there and sell the clothes off your back. The others won't need to, theirs'll be ripped off. Your van's gone: you should've had the breakfast. You're spineless."

"That's true…"

"Why do you hate me?" said Libby, spilling coins and notes on the floor.

"Come on, Lib," said Sally, following Clark to the door.

"I don't," said the woman, "but those two couldn't give a damn. You've no real friends at all." She dragged Libby to the rotting window and threw it open.

Below, the queue had doubled. As Sally and Clark emerged, struggling with the camera, it gathered itself into a crowd and rushed towards them hurling stones and bottles. By the time it had reached them they were a blue coat and an orange coat lying on the ground, the equipment beside them.

"Something happened after all, didn't it?" The woman's voice was loud in Libby's ear. "You're thinking there might be some good footage on that." True, Libby had been thinking just that, but now she couldn't bear to look, as the crowd fell upon the two figures, covering them completely. "They had it coming," the woman said. "Someone'll get that film, wait a few days and sell it to NTV when they start to worry. They'll get a good price. And then everyone will know about Wantwick and how we do things here."

"True…"

"You can stay as long as you like," she added, picking up the coins on the floor and slipping them in the pocket of her dressing gown, "free. I don't mean your keep—you'll have to work for that—just the staying. I'd take advantage of the offer if I were you."

"She's right," said the voice from the cupboard.

"This is what those people pay for?" asked Libby, wiping her eyes. Outside, there was no sign of Clark and Sally. A man strode up to the camera and beckoned to two small girls, who scurried forward and helped him to strap it on his back.

"The people of Wantwick," the woman declared, "are mean as hell but they live to a good age and have a strict regard for truth. Are you staying or are you going out?"

Downstairs, someone impatient was knocking on the door. For the first time, Libby looked the woman properly in the face, and managed for a few seconds to meet her pale grey eyes. "What will I do?" she asked.

The woman pulled one of the animal cages away from the wall and groped for something behind it. "Stay," she replied, holding out a maroon dressing gown festooned with cobwebs, and explained, almost gently: "For when you sell the clothes off your back."

The Kissing Disease

THE VIRUS TO BLAME, much magnified, looked soft and harmless, like a punctured tennis ball. It lived in the salivary glands; the disease could only be transmitted mouth to mouth and children at least were immune till puberty. Gary—who was fourteen—lay on the floor in his bedroom, the door locked to protect him from whoever else was in the house. He was listening to national radio. It was a panel discussion, with various oldies going on about how not kissing was ruining their lives.

"It's all very well," one woman said, her voice quivering with emotion, "to say it's just a little thing, but it's the part of lovemaking I've always enjoyed most, really."

"I'd go further than that," another chipped in. "It's an activity I used to enjoy in its own right, even prefer to, well, you know."

"Let's call a spade a spade," said a third. "It's a charter for the most brutal and demeaning kind of heterosexual sex."

It was amazing, Gary thought, that so many people found it impossible to resist kissing, considering that unless they had some other disease as well it was perfectly possible to do all the rest and anything else you could imagine on top. Maybe they'd made a mistake about the incubation period being only a couple of hours. Or maybe it was just that the older generation had got in the habit and couldn't get out of it, sticking their tongue inside each other's mouths and so on, yuck, getting those saliva glands working a treat. He caressed his prick affectionately: under his jeans it was hard—most of the time these days.

"Surely," said the chairman, "this is all just conditioning. After all, don't we all know that the Eskimos never kiss anyway?"

"Too right!" Gary said, and beat the floor with his fist. Nor did he: he'd grown up with it.

"And we shouldn't forget," the chairman continued solemnly, "that Laverill is far from unique. The sudden emergence of a new virus is now a fact of modern life, with nearly forty towns in this country alone hosting a new contagious disease, each with its own problems and tragedies."

But there were plenty of advantages too, Gary thought. School was still going, but only just. As the teachers went down, they had to bring people in from outside, and some of them didn't last very long: really, you only attended if you wanted to: it was more of a social occasion than education. And there could be no other part of the country where sexual intercourse between minors was regarded as the lesser of two evils, and on top of that, even if it hadn't been, there was no one in a fit state to check up on it…No other place on earth where a fourteen-year-old would be able to put it about with such impunity, and all the schoolgirls were issued with contraceptive pills and condoms. Men didn't like kissing anyway: they liked fucking.

THE TOWN WAS SURROUNDED by a *cordon sanitaire*. The army had thrown up a barbed-wire fence and there were roadblocks, even on the little lanes and byways. From his window Gary could see the fires they lit to keep warm. He wanted to be a soldier himself, when he grew up. It wouldn't be long, perhaps a week, they said on the news, till all children and adults untouched by the disease were evacuated. Once outside, after a period of quarantine, they would be able to kiss without risk. But Gary wasn't at all sure if he wanted to go. He was frightened of kissing, and he liked Laverill: he'd never be so free anywhere else.

He had a photograph of a man and a woman kissing, torn from a magazine. He kept it under his mattress: but he didn't need to get it out in order to see it. He'd looked at it so often that it was printed on his retina. Their eyes were hooded, their faces smooth, slack as those of sleepers. They'd twisted their necks so that their teeth didn't clash, and opened their mouths wide. The woman had her hands in the picture as well: she was holding the man's jaw pulling him closer and down. It was horrible, perverse.

Gary shook his head to get rid of the image, turned the radio off and stood by his door listening: all quiet. He turned the key and slipped down the stairs. He'd go to the pub and have a couple of pints with his best and only friend Tim, a private from one of the regiments guarding Laverill. Gary had met him wandering about the town one night and helped him to find a clean girl. When it came to it, Tim had been reluctant, and Gary had to put his hand on his shoulders and push him forward. But after, Tim said he thought he was in love and wanted to see her again the next night.

"No," Gary explained. "Girls aren't like us. If they do it too often, eventually they go soft and want to kiss you. They're stupid that way."

"But if she's safe…" said Tim.

"But if she does it to you, she'll do it to anyone—and then it's only a matter of time—see?" He'd been proved right. Tim might be in the army, but he had no real experience of girls, and *no idea* what it was like to live in Laverill. His naivety offset the difference in their heights and ages and made the friendship possible.

THERE WERE TWO BARS, one for the kissers—the larger one—and one for the clean. He had to walk past the frosted glass of the kissers' bar. God only knew what was going on in there: there were shouts and laughter, bursts of song, a sudden silence and then a scraping sound as if tables were being moved. As he paused to listen, the lights went off and someone burst out of the door walking on all fours. He hurried around the corner to the clean door.

He showed his card, and recited his address and date of birth. You had to be a member and renew the card after your test, every month: it was a nuisance, but without some check, kissers would always be sneaking in, as if they didn't have the bigger bar for themselves anyway.

Tim was at their usual table in the corner and nodded curtly when Gary raised his eyebrows and pointed at his glass: people were quiet in the clean bar, but the music, whilst drowning out the din from next door, made it almost impossible to hear someone speak from more than a couple of feet away. Tim sat with his shoulders slumped; he had dark circles under his eyes. He took his pint without thanks and downed a good third of it in one go.

"I'm sick of Laverill," he said. "It's doing me in, all this keeping your mouth to yourself. I'll be screwing someone and all I can think of is how my mouth is filling up with saliva. Haven't you noticed that?"

"I just spit," said Gary, taking a mouthful of beer.

"It makes me—you know. I lose it. It's embarrassing." There was a long silence between them. Gary began to tap out the beat of the music on the table, then stopped himself.

"I dream of lips," Tim said quietly, looking at the backs of his hands. Gary exhaled slowly, shaking his head.

"It's different for you because you grew up outside. You must've got the habit of it, I suppose. Me, I never have."

"Exactly what happens, when someone gets it? Does it really rot your brain? That's what they told us in the camp."

"Well, not exactly rot," Gary said slowly and with a certain amount of relish. Despite the subject matter, he

149

enjoyed being the one in the know. "More like *scramble*—I mean, people can still add up, drive cars, even planes, if they want to. Sometimes they do things they couldn't manage before, in fact. Mutating Identity Syndrome. My mum and dad got it, right at the beginning before they knew what it was. Her first; then she gave it to him.

"It doesn't show on the outside. Not at all. She came home one afternoon, just like normal, and pottered around in the kitchen. I was about twelve. She gave me a glass of milk with some digestive biscuits. Then she went upstairs, and I heard her on the phone for a bit. I put the TV on, and I didn't realize at first that the singing was her! Never heard anything like it. I went up, and she was sitting on the edge of her bed in her slip with her hand on her chest like this, singing her heart out. Italian opera. Wavering and swooping up and down, very loud. Her face was the same, but it had an expression on it like I've never seen before: like the cat that's got a lifetime supply of cream. She looked right through me. It wasn't her anymore."

"Was the singing in tune?" asked Tim.

"As far as I can tell. The point is, my mum never sang. Not so much as hummed a theme tune. And there she was…Next thing, there's a hammering on the door. A bloke with a van trying to deliver a piano ordered by Mrs. Canetti. Just as I've persuaded him to go away—the singing blaring out of her window all the while—up comes someone else who says he's her voice tutor. I try to slam the door in his face—I wanted to phone my dad—but he keeps pushing the bell; the singing stops and down she comes in her dressing gown.

"There's no one here of that name," she says. That was it—over, just like that. Snap. Back to normal as if nothing had happened. Whole thing can't have lasted more than an hour. But of course it gets worse. They do it more and more often, and they don't always come back to who they really are in between. Sometimes it's real people, sometimes invented ones. Once she brought a whole lot of other kids back to the house and started giving them baths. Another time she was, well, best not say. You can imagine. They slip into other people's houses, or see a nice car and drive off in it, things like that. And of course, when they're off, they forget they've got it and go around kissing and infecting everyone else. I haven't seen my dad for weeks. Don't want to either, after the last time. Basically, since the age of twelve, I've had to look after myself. Of course, it has advantages...I'd've never got into a pub before, for instance..." Tim sighed, looking around the bar. It was about half-full. The people in it were mostly very young or very old and many of them were sitting alone.

"And I can't wait to be in the army like you," said Gary. "As soon as I can. Solid. Stable." He sat up straighter.

"Only one personality between us, eh?" said Tim. "Fact is, Gary, it's not a lot of fun. I don't really know why we're here. I'm not supposed to tell anyone this," he continued softly, rubbing his chin. "None of the kissers ever try to escape, you know. But every day we turn back hundreds of people trying to get in. Someone was shot in the leg yesterday. It made me sick—an old man with a walking stick, just ignored all warnings—" He emptied his glass and grasped Gary's arm. "Come on. I can't stand this dump. I mean, sounds like they're having a better time on that side than we are here…Let's go out for a bit."

They walked in silence down High Street. For once, most of the street lights were on. It was past nine, but some of the shops were still open and full of people, though they were not always shopping. Some kind of amateur dramatics were taking place in Ransome's; there was an art class in the pharmacy. Other shops had broken windows and nothing left inside; yet others had been unopened for months, their displays thick with dust. The state of the town, too, had its advantages: it was a long time since Gary had paid for anything except food—the grocery store was run by the army—though one day, he supposed, everything would run out. He spotted a couple kissing, slipped his arm through Tim's and steered him over to the other side of the road. Tim could have arrested them if he had his uniform on, but even so Gary would have thought twice before pointing them out; it was just too embarrassing.

"I've had enough of this," he said as soon as they were safely past. "What about the Fox and Grapes just up there?"

"*We* could—" Tim began, stopping in his tracks.

"Could what?"

"You know. Kiss." Gary's arm was still threaded through his.

"Get off me! You've got it!" he shouted, trying to pull away but only succeeding in twisting his shoulder.

"Hold on," said Tim, "I haven't. I'm Tim Murray, right? It's just I miss it. And you ought at least to know what it's like."

"It's disgusting," said Gary and spat copiously on the pavement.

"It'd be safe. Just once." Very slowly, Tim removed his hands from his pockets, thus releasing Gary's arm. They stood, facing each other in a silence punctuated only by the sharp intake of their breath and the helpless sound Gary made when he swallowed. Tim slipped one hand gently behind his neck. Gary felt as if he was going to faint—the erection was easily the biggest he'd ever had—and as Tim's face moved closer, he moved his body back so that it wouldn't be detected. Their lips touched, warm and dry but terribly soft; there was a moment's hesitation, then Gary closed his eyes and twisted his neck a little—it happened without thinking—his jaw relaxed, and Tim's tongue slipped inside, running between teeth and lips, nudging against the roof to this mouth. He couldn't speak; but he thought *God*, and wanted to do it back. They drew breath and began again, slower. Their lips were wet now, mobile and slippery. Gary clasped Tim to him, and subsided against the window of a shop that once sold greetings cards.

"Let's stop for a bit," he gasped after he didn't know how long. He was exhausted and his lips felt raw.

"Okay," said Tim. They walked on, side by side, more slowly than before.

"Here it is," Tim said. "The Fox and Grapes." Gary didn't notice at first that they'd passed the entrance to the clean bar. Tim passed briefly outside the door marked with a roughly painted 'K', which was ajar. He raised his eyebrows just as if he were asking whether Gary wanted another pint.

My Fees

NO ONE CAN HEAR US and the room is plain, scarcely lit, warmed to the temperature of blood. I listen. I hear the way your voice rises or tightens or softens when you are not telling the truth. Other signs tell me whether or not you are aware of your own self-deception. I watch. I see the small tensions of the face, a quiver of the eyelids, one hand slipping up to cover the mouth, your eyes suddenly sliding to the side, as if reading posters from a moving train. I read your clothes. Why do you never dress warmly enough? Why do you always choose such clear colours, such stiff fabrics, so much black? Why is everything too loose or too tight and what is the story of that small golden brooch pinned on the left side, right above the heart?

I see the body beneath its coverings, how the vertebrae in the middle of your spine bear too heavily down on each other. I notice worn hands or smooth ones, bitten nails, the sudden angle of your foot, weak arms, asymmetrical musculature. I know whether there is a void or a fire between your legs, whether you are bleeding, that your throat hurts, your stomach churns. I can tell from the way you sit which parts of your body you will not look at; that you will be disgusted by hair growing through skin or in love with your own slenderness or with the raised scar on your arm. But none of this, not the room itself, neither the listening nor the watching are the reason for the fee.

Beyond the body is landscape: ranges of mountains you have climbed, up above the snow into a zone of purple-white air or strange moonscapes of rock, or thick cedar-smelling forest where no light reaches the softly rotting floor; Mediterranean islands; a desert; pink hills with old cities perched on their sides; moors sprung with heather; flat fields beneath a sky of towering cloud; a beach with white sand and spangled turquoise sea.

I understand that we all speak poetry. You may talk about a room that seems too small or too large, too dark, too cramped, too bright, too fussy, too red. Or it might be that you long for a kitchen painted white with just a wooden table and a chair. You may describe a fortified castle with arrow slits for windows, very forbidding, the stone dark with constantly falling rain. Or else a garden full of fruit hanging on the trees just beyond reach. You may hate cities or long for them, the same with thunderstorms. You may tell me of your violent dislikes towards people you meet or how you have fallen in love with a stranger because of the sound of his or